Crooked Wood

by the same author

A PINCH OF SNUFF
THE JUROR
MENACES, MENACES
MURDER WITH MALICE
THE FATAL TRIP

CROOKED WOOD

Michael Underwood

ST. MARTIN'S PRESS
NEW YORK

Library of Congress Cataloging in Publication Data

Underwood, Michael, 1916–
    Crooked wood.

    I. Title
PZ4.E94Ct   1978   [PR6055.V3]   823'.9'14   77–14662
ISBN 0–312–17653–8

'From such crooked wood as that which man is made of, nothing straight can be fashioned.'

Kant

PROLOGUE

She had received him with hostility which had increased as his visit proceeded. She had said little. She had had no need to. Her eyes and the set of her mouth conveyed her feelings toward him.

He could now feel her hostility at his back as he walked down the narrow hall. Nevertheless, he turned on reaching the front-door as if to give her a final opportunity of acknowledging that he might, after all, have a point of view worth considering. But her expression made further words futile. With a slight shrug, he stepped across the threshold and she immediately closed the door behind him as though putting another shutter between them.

He shivered, only partly from the icy draught which blew along the outside corridor, and hurried, shoulders hunched, toward the lift. He pressed the button and waited impatiently, but nothing happened. Then he heard running footsteps on the stone stairs, followed by laughter and a string of adolescent obscenities.

He realised that some children had just put it out of action, doubtless for the umpteenth time that month.

He set off down the stairs, thankful that he had only four floors to descend. God help any old folk who lived in the higher reaches of the block. They must spend half their lives marooned above the world.

He emerged at the bottom on to the asphalt surround which was still euphemistically referred to as landscaping by those who received the constant stream of tenants' complaints and felt obliged to fight back.

It was like walking across a barrack square and he quickened his step for the wind was no less cold at ground level than it had been whistling through the building's corridors.

A low wall surrounded the three tower blocks and he made for the gap nearest which he had parked his car.

He reached the car and was about to unlock the driver's door, when, out of the corner of his eye, he glimpsed a tiny spurt of flame. At the same time there was a muffled explosion, but, before his mind could register this, the bullet had smashed its way into his head.

CHAPTER ONE

Police informers are generally unloved and, looking at Gordy Warren, Nick Attwell could easily see why. He was small and wiry, with a narrow head and a smile that sent your hand to your wallet to make sure it was still there. His pale, watery eyes were never still and his soft, warm breath was surprisingly harmless. Nick was particularly grateful for this as Gordy was one of those people who liked to push his face right against yours when he spoke.

Unloved and despised as they may be, a great many crimes would go unsolved but for the bits of information they impart to police. Their motives are seldom other than venal, but no police force could effectively function without them.

Every C.I.D. officer has his informer with whom he develops a working relationship in which faith is tempered by wariness and rewards are doled out like morsels of fish to performing seals.

In the twelve months or so that Nick had known Gordy Warren, he had received from him a number of tip-offs which had proved reliable and consequently helpful. But none had been as important as that which had led to the arrest of Clive Donig on a charge of murdering Stanley Fulmer.

The trial was due to begin at the Old Bailey on the following day, with Gordy Warren well out of sight and his vital disclosures veiled in anonymity.

'I've never let you down yet, 'ave I, sarge?' he said in a soft, wheedling tone as he leaned across the narrow ledge of a table in the small café where they were meeting. 'Anyway, why should I invent it?' he went on in a faintly aggrieved tone. 'Every time I meet you, sarge, I'm running a risk. It's only because I want to 'elp the police I do it.'

'You'll be telling me next you do it for love,' Nick said with a laugh. Gordy shook his head in sorrowful reproach and Nick went on, 'Anyway, I'm not doubting your information; what I need to know is how reliable it is.'

''Ave I ever not been reliable?' Gordy asked in his self-pitying voice.

'You've got to find out more, and quickly, too. You've got to. At the moment it's all too vague. Oh, we'll take it seriously all right, but there's little we can do unless you can come up with something stronger. A name, that's what I want, Gordy. A name.'

Gordy Warren examined a bitten thumb-nail with a faintly sulky expression. 'Most officers I know would 'ave given the earth for that bit of information,' he said. 'If it 'adn't been for me, you wouldn't be 'aving a Bailey trial. You'd never 'ave got on to Donig without my 'elp. Now own up, sarge, that's the truth and you knows it.'

Nick let out a sigh. He wondered how many more times they would go through this well-worn routine. Whenever Gordy felt dissatisfied with his treatment, which was as regular as phases of the moon, he would remind Nick of all his past services.

'Let's hear the other side, Gordy. I know that side by heart.'

'What other side?'

'The side that tells of all the advantages which have come your way. I know you expect the Commissioner to find you a nice, cosy pad and pay your board and lodging for the rest of your life *and* keep you supplied with those big bosomy birds you go for, but forget all that and count your blessings.'

'Blessings!'

'If you can find out a bit more, I'll see that you're decently rewarded.'

''Ow much?'

'It could be worth quite a bit.'

'A cent?'

'Yes, it could be worth a hundred. *If* it proves reliable. But you've got to find out more.'

'Aren't you going to give me anything for what I already told you?'

Nick reached into his pocket and produced the two £10 notes he had brought along. 'On account,' he said, passing them over.

With almost sleight of hand, the notes disappeared into one of Gordy's pockets.

'Call me at home this evening if you find anything out. Otherwise we'll meet here to-morrow after court. Say about seven o'clock, in case I have to stay on and confer with counsel. And if I want to get in touch with you in the course of the day, I'll phone the pub.'

Gordy Warren had part-time employment as a cellarman in a public house in Camden Town where an indulgent licensee allowed him the use of an attic room rent-free.

As they got up to leave, Gordy appeared to emerge from the brooding mood into which he had sunk.

' 'Ow's your kid, sarge?'

'Simon? He's fine.'

'Tell 'im, I'm going to give 'im a present. It's a surprise. 'Ow old is 'e, did you say?'

'Three.'

'I'd like to 'ave 'ad a son,' Gordy remarked wistfully.

Nick said nothing, but tried to envisage the sort of offspring Gordy Warren and one of his bosomy lady friends might produce. He decided that it might be very odd-looking, with its father's narrow head and mother's probable mammary proportions.

Gordy had been on about giving Simon a present for several months, but to Nick's relief, the matter had never got any further. He had no wish to become beholden to his informer in that way; on the other hand, the refusal of an actually proffered gift was an embarrassment he hoped to be spared.

As Nick walked away from their rendezvous, he reflected that he would obviously inform prosecuting counsel first thing next morning of what Gordy Warren had told him. And that was about all he could do. His own superior officer in the case was lying on a hospital bed slowly recovering from an operation for a slipped disc which had felled him soon after most of the major work in the enquiry had been accomplished. Nick had accordingly been left on his own in the run-up to trial stage of the case, though with Detective Superintendent Peter Bramber to turn to in the event of necessity. Nick did not regard it as necessary to bother him yet. He would await counsel's reaction, it being primarily a counsel matter. He would also discuss it with Clare when he got home that evening. That was the boon of having a wife who had once been a police officer herself. She was not only interested in his cases, but could also view them with a professional eye.

It was half past eight before he arrived back at the small house in Barnes where they lived.

Clare, who had been watching television, came into the hall to greet him as she always did.

'Hello, darling. Ready to eat?'

'Too right. I'm ravenous,' he said, after they had kissed. 'I'll just go upstairs and have a wash.'

Clare knew that taking a peep at Simon rated considerably higher with Nick than having a wash. She sometimes reflected how much better balanced their lives would be if they could take equal turns at minding Simon and doing police work. Not that she had ever regretted quitting in order to get married – or, rather, to marry Nick. On the other hand she had never been averse to helping him in practical fashion with one of his cases when the opportunity had arisen. The fact that such help had to be hidden and unofficial usually added zest to the occasion.

Upstairs Nick stood looking down at his sleeping son. Simon lay breathing quietly, his arms outside the covers as though ready for instant use. He had always resisted having them tucked in. His light brown hair had been recently cut and, to his father at any rate, he now looked a real little boy. Not that he had ever given much evidence of being anything else.

Nick blew him a silent kiss and crept out of the bedroom.

'All set for to-morrow?' Clare enquired as he came into the kitchen.

'Except that Gordy Warren's thrown a potential spanner into the works. He called me earlier to-day and said he must see me urgently as he'd picked up a vital straw affecting the trial.' Clare paused, casserole dish in hand, half-way between oven and table and waited for Nick to go on. 'He says an attempt is going to be made to nobble the jury.'

'Which way?'

'Need you ask. To secure Donig's acquittal.'

'Who's going to do the nobbling?'

'That's what I've told Gordy to find out. He didn't know.'

'And you believe him?'

'Does one ever believe anything Gordy tells one unless it can be checked out!'

'Where'd he learn this?'

'He says he overheard a conversation between two men in the pub where he works.'

'And he doesn't know who the men are, I suppose,' Clare observed, sardonically.

'That's what he says. He'd not seen them there previously. He heard the name, Donig, mentioned as he passed by and so he tuned in on their conversation as well as he could without actually appearing to eavesdrop.'

'Seems unlikely he'd have invented it.'

'That's what I think.'

'Of course, it's a long leap from trying to nobble a jury to achieving it.'

'Yes, though it still happens.'

'Presumably, no one knows at this moment who the jurors will be in the Donig case.'

'That's why all I can do is to let prosecuting counsel know and leave him to challenge anyone who may look susceptible to being nobbled. After all, he and I are as likely to recognise the type as whoever it is waiting in the shadows to do the nobbling.' He speared a lump of meat on his fork and put it into his mouth.

'Forewarned is forearmed,' Clare said, starting to eat. 'Particularly in that realm. Can't the judge be persuaded to say something in open court? If he told the jury to report any improper approaches, the nobbler might well be frightened off.'

'Provided we don't empanel a bad apple, without being aware of the fact.'

'That's where you and counsel's powers of perception will come in.' She chewed for a while, looking thoughtful. Then with a small hesitant smile, she said, 'I could get along for an hour to-morrow. Sally's picking Simon up from play-school and giving him lunch. Alexander's coming here the next day.' Alexander was currently Simon's best friend.

Nick's expression told Clare all she needed to know.

'That's a great idea,' he said. 'Even if you can't shout out "Don't have *him*", you'll be able to tell me afterwards which of them you thought looked dodgy. Feminine intuition and all that.'

'Yes,' Clare said, 'it'll be interesting to try and do that. Also to spot the nobbler himself. He's bound to be in court.'

'More likely a henchman.'

'Who's defending Donig?'

'Julius Orkell, Q.C., with Barry Gand as his junior.'

'Who are his solicitors?'

'Naseby and Co.'

'Reputable?'

'I gather so.'

'Not like Fulmer and Co.?' Clare remarked with a smile.

Nick grinned. 'Even they could scarcely defend the man who'd murdered their senior partner.'

CHAPTER TWO

'Bernard Smith . . . Arthur Perkins . . . Barbara Anderson . . .
Ephraim Clavering-Jones . . .'

As each name was intoned by the clerk of the court, its
owner took his place in the jury box and came under the
immediate scrutiny of Nick and Robin Mendip, the Treasury
Counsel nominated to prosecute in the case. Somewhere behind
both of them sat Clare, also intently studying each new face
as the jury box slowly filled.

So far they looked just about as ordinary as their names,
save that Ephraim Clavering-Jones appeared more so than his.
He was a tall, handsome negro who managed to look rather
more relaxed than his colleagues.

At last the jury box was full, nine men and three women.
As Nick ran his eye along the two rows, he decided that there
was only one whose looks he didn't care for. Trevor Lee in the
middle of the back row. It wasn't his open-neck red shirt and
black corduroy jacket that affronted Nick's idea of how a
juror should dress, nor his shoulder-length ungroomed hair, for
jurors came in all sizes, colours and descriptions these days. It
was his mean mouth and arrogant stare that made Nick turn
and whisper to Mr Mendip.

'Don't like the look of him, sir. Can't we get him off?'

'We'll wait and see how the defence play it,' counsel whispered back.

When Nick had told him and Tom Parrod, the junior
prosecuting counsel, of Gordy's tip-off, Robin Mendip had
said they would have to play it by ear, though he would
certainly mention it in open court before the end of the day
so that the judge could warn the jury to be on their guard
against any improper approaches.

As to challenging any jurors whom they didn't like the look
of, he reminded Nick that this had become an increasingly
sensitive area for the crown, with certain politicians always

15

ready to use it as a stick with which to belabour the existing system. If the defence made a number of challenges, it was easier for the crown to do so. But if the defence made none, then, unless they had real cause, discretion required the crown to sit tight and hope for the best. He had also pointed out that it was too late to have a jury check – a check, that is, of all the names on the list from which the jury would be selected – and, moreover, even if it had not been too late, it was unlikely to have been sanctioned in this particular case. Nick had nodded, aware that this was yet another fetter which had recently been imposed on the prosecuting authority in the alleged interest of fairness. Fairness to the defence had become a strident and distorted cry which often drowned the less articulate plea of society as a whole for protection from wrong-doers.

Nick turned back and surveyed again the object of his disquiet. Trevor Lee was sitting back with arms folded across his chest and an expression of imperious disdain on his face. He was the prototype anti-police demonstrator, it was written all over him. He would be in favour of an acquittal simply because he could never appear to ally himself with those who represented law and order.

Nick's thoughts were interrupted by the clerk of the court telling the accused that the jurors selected to try him were about to be sworn and that, if he wished to object to any of them, he must do so when their names were called and before they were sworn.

Donig threw his counsel a quick glance and received a reassuring nod.

To Nick's dismay, the six in the front row were sworn without challenge. The first three in the back row went similarly unchallenged and then the Testament was handed to Trevor Lee. Nick turned his head to give counsel a last despairing look, but Robin Mendip merely gave him a wink and a slight shrug.

Nick's worst fears were confirmed when Trevor Lee declined to take an oath, but said condescendingly that he would affirm.

Nick had almost lost interest when Mr Orkell suddenly called out, 'Challenge.' The juror in question, a somewhat formidable-looking lady named Judith Walker, froze in apparent indignation and glared at defending counsel who wisely looked elsewhere.

'Would you mind leaving the box, madam?' the judge said with a small apologetic smile.

Julius Orkell leaned sideways and murmured to Robin Mendip, 'I thought she looked a bit too much like the president of the Hang'em and Flog'em Society.'

Mendip grinned. 'Probably find she's as soft as melted ice-cream underneath.'

Judith Walker was replaced by William Smythe, whose looks couldn't have offended anyone. He was small and nondescript with a bald head and a moustache grown to compensate for the absence of hair on his head. Or so it seemed to Clare.

If she had been able to communicate her views to anyone, they would have been that, though Trevor Lee looked the obvious trouble-maker, there were others whose exteriors might well prove to be deceptively stolid and respectable. It seemed to her that it would be a waste of anyone's time to try and nobble Trevor Lee. It would be like preaching to the converted. As for Ephraim Clavering-Jones, she thought he looked one of the more intelligent jurors. Once or twice he had whispered something to one of his neighbours and had revealed a pleasant, easy smile and a general air of alertness.

Clare turned her attention back to the accused sitting in the huge dock of Number 1 Court. He looked less thuggish than Nick had led her to believe. Perhaps because he so obviously was one, she had expected him to resemble one more. Apart from his rather squashed nose, he had good, strong features. Short fair hair, a firm jaw-line and cornflower-blue eyes. He certainly had a tough, chunky appearance as befitted someone who had boxed for his regiment. But then he had been court-martialled for striking a sergeant-major in the orderly room, knocking him out cold at that, and had been dismissed the service, since when he had lived by crime, generally as the strong-arm man in any enterprise requiring one. According to Nick, he was a killer by instinct, acting without emotion. He certainly exhibited none as he sat in the dock with an expression carved from stone.

She looked from Donig to the man facing him across the well of the court. Mr Justice Finderson was a new judge and

little was known of him. His wig and scarlet robes might indicate that his appointment was recent, but Clare felt that anyone who sought to take advantage of the fact could well find
themselves judicially gored. In his own way, he looked every
bit as tough as the accused in the dock.

The jury had been sworn, the indictment had been read to
the accused who had pleaded not guilty in an expressionless
voice and Clare sat back in her seat as Robin Mendip rose to
open the case.

'May it please your lordship, members of the jury, I appear
to prosecute in this case with my learned friend Mr Parrod
and the accused, Clive Donig, is represented by my learned
friends, Mr Orkell and Mr Gand.

'As you have heard, members of the jury, the charge is one
of murder, the allegation being that the accused murdered
Stanley Fulmer on the eighth of January this year. As you will
in due course be directed by my lord, it is for the prosecution
to prove the charge. To prove beyond reasonable doubt that
the accused did what the prosecution alleges, namely that he
murdered Stanley Fulmer. There are a number of unusual
features about the case, but, leaving those on one side for a
moment, there is, in the prosecution's submission, clear evidence to prove the charge to your satisfaction.

'When you have heard all the evidence, you may well reach
the conclusion that this was what is called a contract murder.
Namely that someone wanted Mr Fulmer killed and employed,
directly or indirectly, the accused to carry out the deed. In a
word, the accused was a hired killer. He killed Mr Fulmer
because he was paid to do so.'

Prosecuting counsel turned a page of his notebook, gave his
gown a hitch and went on, 'Stanley Fulmer was a solicitor,
members of the jury, the senior partner in the firm of Fulmer
and Co. which has an office in Crenly Street, just off Totten-
ham Court Road. Mr Fulmer's practice was primarily in the
criminal law and he was a well-known figure in this and other
criminal courts.' Mendip glanced along the row to where a
small, hunched counsel was scribbling furiously in a notebook.
This was Mr Tagg who was holding a watching brief on behalf
of the victim's late firm. His role gave him no voice in the
proceedings, but Mendip reckoned that he would have quite a

busy time reporting back on the various imputations that were likely to be made once the defence got going.

'On the eighth of January,' counsel went on, 'Mr Fulmer was shot through the head beside the driver's door of his car which was parked outside Medina Towers, a complex of flats in the East End of London. The car door was still locked and the keys were on the ground close by. The car engine was cold. I mention that, members of the jury, because it is the strongest indication that Mr Fulmer had just returned to his car when he was shot rather than that he had just got out of it. This is supported, moreover, by the evidence of a Miss Kitching who lives in the north block of Medina Towers and who recalls looking out of her window and seeing the car parked there about eight o'clock. The murder took place near enough round twenty past eight. That was when the shot was heard and a 999 call was made to the police.'

He paused and pursed his lips in apparent thought for a moment. 'You will probably agree, members of the jury, that the strong inference from what I have told you is that Mr Fulmer had returned to his car after visiting somebody in Medina Towers. There are no fewer than two hundred and forty flats in Medina Towers. Eighty in each of three blocks. Four flats on each floor and twenty floors to each block.' He paused again and fixed the jury with a head-on look. 'The police have called on the occupiers of each of those two hundred and forty flats. In addition they have visited every house within a quarter of a mile of where Mr Fulmer's car was found. No one, but no one, admits to having received a visit from the deceased solicitor that evening. Moreover, despite well publicised appeals, no one has come forward with any information which would explain what he was doing in that area, far from his office and even further from his own home. Mr Penfold, his junior partner in the firm, who left the office around six on the evening in question, will tell you that Mr Fulmer was still at work and said nothing about going to visit anyone in Medina Towers. Mrs Fulmer will tell you that her husband said he wouldn't be home until around nine o'clock that evening, but that there was nothing unusual about that. So what was Mr Fulmer doing in the area of Medina Towers around eight o'clock? The prosecution cannot tell you. He was there all right, there can be no doubt about that. Shot through the head, the bullet lodging in his brain. A bullet fired from a Smith and Wesson .38 revolver.'

From the rapt expressions on the faces of the jurors, it was clear that Robin Mendip had hooked them with his recital of the facts. There was nothing like a murder case with some of its mystery unsolved, Nick reflected as he looked at their faces. Even Trevor Lee couldn't help appearing interested.

'Whoever fired the shot, members of the jury, disappeared without trace immediately afterwards. It was a cold night and the street was deserted. One or two people thought they heard running footsteps after the shot, but no one was observed leaving the scene of the crime. The odds are that the murderer had escaped down a side street almost before anyone could look out of a window. One may presume he had a getaway car conveniently parked in the vicinity. A matter of speculation is where he waited for Mr Fulmer to return to his car. When you come to examine the album of photographs, you will see that almost opposite where the car was parked is a builder's yard with a recessed entrance. It would undoubtedly provide excellent cover for anyone wishing to keep watch and stay out of sight. For two days, the police remained baffled and then certain information reached them. As a result of that information, they went to an address in Hackney where the accused, Donig, was living. In his room they found a Smith and Wesson .38 revolver and £2000 in used notes. The revolver has been examined by a firearms expert at the Metropolitan Police Laboratory who will tell you that he has no doubt it is the weapon which fired the bullet recovered from Mr Fulmer's brain. As to the £2000 found in a carrier bag in a cupboard of his room, the accused said they were his winnings at gambling. However, when pressed, he was unable to give any details as to how or where he had won the money. You may think, members of the jury, that if his story was true, he would have been very quick to have provided details so that the police could check them and confirm what he had said. As it is, coupled with his possession of the revolver, you may well infer that the £2000 was his payment for murdering Mr Fulmer. If that inference is correct, the prosecution is unable to take the matter any further. There is clear evidence that Mr Fulmer

met his death at the hands of the accused. The fact that someone else may have ordered it to happen does not relieve Donig
of his responsibility. I would urge you most strongly, members
of the jury, to concentrate on the facts and not embark on
speculative theories, tempting though it may be. There is no
evidence that the accused and his victim knew each other or
had ever been linked together in any way. It follows that the
accused had no known motive to kill Mr Fulmer, which is why
the prosecution has branded the crime a contract murder.
Happily hired killers are still a rarity in this country, but they
do exist, members of the jury. They do exist.'

'Will you be calling yourself as an expert witness on the
subject, Robin?' Mr Orkell asked in a murmured aside.

The judge frowned and defending counsel quickly buried
his head in his papers. Mendip, who had been about to make
an appropriate riposte, stifled the urge and proceeded to that
part of his opening which required him to expound in greater
detail on the evidence which the prosecution's witnesses would
be called to give.

Nick took the opportunity to slip out of court and check
that all the witnesses who had been warned for attendance
that day had in fact turned up. He had left Detective Constable Cambridge to take care of this aspect.

Ted Cambridge, a keen young officer who played hockey
for the Metropolitan Police, was peering through the glass
panel of the door into court as Nick came out.

'Going all right?' he asked, with the anxious air of an
expectant father.

Nick nodded. 'I reckon Mr Mendip will be about another
half hour. Everyone here?'

'Yes, including Mr Penfold.'

'I thought we'd arranged to phone him, so that he didn't
have to hang around all day.'

'That's right, we did; because he kept reminding us what
a busy man he was and stressing all the extra work he had as
a result of old Fulmer's death.'

'So why's he here now?' Nick asked in a tone of slight
exasperation. Only the police knew what a chore it was getting
witnesses to court. They grumbled at the inconvenience and
had to be cajoled and mollified. In order to mitigate the

inconvenience to busy, professional men, it was often arranged that they should be on the end of a telephone and be summoned to court only at the last minute. Nick had made such an arrangement with Neil Penfold and now, after all that, he had turned up before the trial was scarcely under way.

'He apparently felt it was his duty to keep Mrs Fulmer company. He told me that, on reflection, he didn't think it'd look very good if she had to sit about all day while her late husband's junior partner received star treatment.'

Nick let out a derisive snort. As far as he was concerned, Penfold had been a pain in the arse from the outset. Though he had avoided being downright obstructive, he had certainly not shown the degree of co-operation the police had hoped for and expected. This had been particularly apparent when they had been probing Fulmer's list of clients to try and ascertain whether any of them bore him a grudge and might have felt they had a score to settle. Penfold's attitude had been one of extreme caution and wariness as he withdrew behind a shield of professional privilege and repeatedly stressed the sanctity of a solicitor's relationship with a client. As a result the police had been frustrated in their hopes of examining Stanley Fulmer's records and correspondence. Such bits of information as had come their way had been like autumn leaves blown beneath a door.

Nick glanced past Ted Cambridge to where a number of the witnesses were sitting. Neil Penfold and Brenda Fulmer appeared to be deep in conversation while another woman leaned across listening.

Anticipating Nick's question, D.C. Cambridge said, 'That's Olive Tishman, Mrs Fulmer's sister.'

Nick saw that there was a resemblance between the two women. He knew that Brenda Fulmer was 37, fifteen years younger than her late husband, and he reckoned that Mrs Tishman was the older of the two, probably by two or three years. He watched her with interest. So that was Frank Tishman's wife. In the course of their enquiries they had learnt that Tishman had amassed a fortune in various speculative deals, at least one of which had been the subject of investigation by the Fraud Squad, though nothing came of it, and, more interestingly, that he was rumoured to have cast adulterous eyes at his sister-in-law.

This was something that Fulmer's secretary had told them under seal of great secrecy. Whether or not there was any truth in it, she didn't pretend to know, though it seemed that Stanley Fulmer himself had had his suspicions.

There had certainly not been enough to justify tackling Tishman, who, it was known, flatly refused to see police officers other than in the presence of his legal advisers.

Catching sight of Nick, Penfold got up and came across to where the two officers were standing.

'Good morning, Sergeant Attwell. I decided that I might as well make a complete wreck of my day and be at your disposal.' Nick noticed that the solicitor's hands had a slight tremble which he had not observed before. 'Quite frankly,' Penfold went on, 'I wouldn't have been able to get any work done if I had stayed in the office. My nerves are all to pieces this morning.'

'I'd have thought you were the last person to have nerves about coming to court,' Nick said, with an absence of sympathy.

'It's coming as a witness. I've never given evidence before other than in formal matters.'

'I don't see that you have much to worry about,' Nick said. 'Mr Mendip'll nurse you along.'

'Mendip doesn't worry me, it's Orkell's cross-examination I'm not looking forward to.' Nick, who had been well aware of this, said nothing. 'Have you any idea yet what line the defence is going to take?'

'I imagine they'll seek to show that Mr Fulmer had a lot of enemies as a result of his contacts with the criminal world and that various people might have been glad to see him dead.'

Penfold nodded unhappily. 'Just what I'm afraid of.'

'It's something you haven't been exactly helpful over,' Nick remarked.

'I couldn't be. I'd have been guilty of professional misconduct.'

'The result is,' Nick went on, 'that the defence may have unearthed things in the woodshed which you've hidden from us. Donig may never have been a client of your firm, but he'll certainly have mixed with people whom Mr Fulmer has represented, people who mayn't be too scrupulous about flinging the dirt about.' Nick shrugged. 'Anyway, it's too late to do anything about it now.'

Neil Penfold's mouth turned down in distaste. 'I know the police don't have a very high opinion of my firm, but we do the job we're paid to do.'

Nick gave him a disarming grin. 'You do a very effective job,' he said. He refrained from adding that it was the firm's integrity he held in low opinion, not their efficiency. He felt almost sorry for Penfold, standing there, a neat, well-dressed monument to anxious misery. Almost, but not quite. Although he had never been viewed by the police with the same hostile suspicion that his senior partner attracted, the fact remained that he was associated with the firm. But stripped of the devil's horns which this association gave him in the eyes of the police, he was a rather ordinary, pleasant-looking man of forty with dark wavy hair and a full, firm mouth. Nick gathered that he had been taken on by Stanley Fulmer to deal with their non-criminal work. Even Fulmer and Co.'s clients apparently bought and sold houses, divorced their wives and made wills, none of which legal work was to Mr Fulmer's taste.

D.C. Cambridge darted from Nick's side to speak to a witness who was semaphoring him from the far side of the great marble hall and Nick and Penfold strolled across to where Mrs Fulmer and her sister were sitting. Brenda Fulmer was wearing a burgundy red coat with a black velvet collar.

'I hope the judge won't expect to see me in widow's weeds,' she said, as Nick approached. 'At least I'm not wearing trousers. I read the other day of some stuffy judge who gave an unfortunate woman hell because she turned up to give evidence in trousers. What on earth's wrong with a woman wearing trousers in court? They cover much more of her than some skirts would. You're not conservative about these things, are you, Mr Attwell?' she asked with a coquettish smile.

'I don't think so,' Nick said, wondering if Clare would agree. On occasions, she labelled him conventional male, a tag which he usually indignantly repudiated.

'By the way, this is my sister, Mrs Tishman.'

Nick shook hands with the older woman. The family resemblance was more apparent at close quarters, though Olive Tishman was larger and had taken less care of her figure.

'Will it be all right for me to come into court when Brenda gives evidence?' she asked.

'Certainly. I'll get D.C. Cambridge to find you a seat.'

It did not seem to Nick that there was any element of constraint between the two sisters which indicated either than the rumour about Frank Tishman casting covetous eyes at his sister-in-law was false or that Olive Tishman was wholly ignorant of the fact.

Turning to both his witnesses, Nick said, 'When you've completed your evidence, I'll get Mr Mendip to ask if you can be released. That is, if you so wish.'

'I'd certainly be glad to get away,' Penfold said.

'I don't mind staying,' Mrs Fulmer said, as though bestowing a favour. 'In fact, I'd quite like to.' Noticing Nick's expression, she added, 'I can see I've surprised you, if not actually shocked you. But Stanley's murder took place five months ago. I'm no longer a newly bereaved widow. Moreover, I feel I owe it to him to hear a bit of the trial of the man who killed him. There's nothing very shocking about that, is there?'

'Put like that, I don't suppose there is,' Nick remarked, though still of the view that most women would not choose to do so in similar circumstances. Addressing Neil Penfold, he said, 'Then I'll ask Mr Mendip to request your release when you've finished. I don't expect the defence will object.'

D.C. Cambridge came over to say that prosecuting counsel had just finished his opening and, with a brief parting word, Nick hurried back into court. As he made his way to his seat, he glanced toward the back of the court-room where Clare was sitting and they exchanged fleeting smiles.

So far as the prosecution was concerned, Brenda Fulmer's evidence was short and uncontroversial and Mendip would have been prepared to dispense with her attendance and to have had her statement read to the jury. The defence, however, had given notice that they wished her to come and testify in person.

While she was taking the oath, the judge appeared to study her with undue, if dispassionate, interest, rather as a white slaver might assess the commercial prospects of a new girl.

25

Replacing the bible and pulling her glove back on, she proceeded to return his interest with one faintly arched eyebrow so that he quickly turned his head away.

Robin Mendip elicited from her that she had been married to Stanley Fulmer for ten years, that they lived in a flat in Delbury Mansions off Edgware Road and that they had no children. She went on to tell the court that when her husband left to go to his office on the morning of January the eighth, he had said he wouldn't be home until about nine o'clock that evening. He hadn't said why he would be late and she hadn't asked him. She accepted it was a business matter. Before she had had time to become really worried about his non-return, the police had called round with news of his death. In answer to counsel's further question, she said she had no idea what had taken him to Medina Towers. She certainly didn't know anyone who lived there; indeed, she had never previously heard of the place.

When Julius Orkell rose to cross-examine her, she shifted her stance slightly to face him and rested her folded hands on the ledge in front of her. Nick, who was watching her, couldn't help admiring her composure. Her black hair was beautifully set and she resembled a fashion model before the cameras rather than someone about to face the ordeal of cross-examination.

For a few seconds, defending counsel stared at her over the top of his half-spectacles, then leaning forward and placing his fingertips delicately on the bulwark of books in front of him, he said, 'Would it be true to say, Mrs Fulmer, that you knew very little about your husband's professional activities?'

'Yes, it would, Mr Orkell,' she replied in a tone which seemed to carry a note of congratulation to counsel for asking such an astute question.

'He never discussed his clients with you, for example?'

'Never.'

'You knew, of course, that he represented a great number of criminals?'

'I couldn't help knowing that.'

'But your husband wouldn't talk about them in detail, is that right?'

'Quite right.'

'Did he ever mention names at all?'

'He might do so occasionally, but they never stuck in my mind.'

'Did clients ever visit him after office hours at your flat in Delbury Mansions?'

'From time to time.'

'Would you meet them on such occasions?'

She shook her head. 'No. My husband would let them in and take them into his study. I never saw them at all.'

'Did you ever wonder why clients came to your flat?'

She raised her eyebrows in faint surprise. 'No. I imagine it was for convenience' sake. There's nothing very unusual about it, is there?'

'I'm afraid I can only ask questions, not answer them,' Mr Orkell said with a wisp of a smile.

Mrs Fulmer gave a small shrug, as if to indicate she hadn't begun the silly game, and glanced toward the judge for support. He declined to look up, however, and continued writing in his notebook.

Mr Orkell bent further forward and fixed the witness with an intent gaze. 'Do you have any knowledge of your husband receiving threats, Mrs Fulmer?'

'Threats?' she echoed with a frown.

'Yes, threats. Threats to his person?'

'I believe there was one occasion,' she said slowly.

'You say you believe, Mrs Fulmer. Did your husband tell you so?'

'I suppose he must have done.'

'Surely it's something you'd remember?'

'I recall now, he did tell me.'

'Was that in case the person concerned called at the flat?'

'Probably.'

'Did your husband report these threats to the police?'

'I couldn't tell you.'

'At all events, no police officer ever came to see you?'

'That's correct.'

'Are we talking about threats by one of the deceased's clients, Mr Orkell?' the judge broke in.

'Yes, my lord.'

Mr Justice Finderson pursed his lips in a thoughtful expression. Then turning to face the witness, he said, 'Was your husband ever assaulted in connection with these threats, Mrs Fulmer?'

'Not as far as I know.'

'It seems reasonable to suppose that you would have known.'

'I agree, my lord.'

Turning his attention back to counsel, he said, 'I'm not clear where this is taking us, Mr Orkell.'

'It all shows, my lord, that the deceased had enemies. Enemies, moreover, in the criminal fraternity.'

'Yes, well . . . I'm not too sure how relevant this all is to the issues the jury will have to consider and I hope you're not going too far out on a tangent, Mr Orkell.'

'I certainly have no wish to do that, my lord, and I'm grateful for your lordship's words.' Counsel gave his gown a pluck and went on, 'I'd like to put a name to the witness, my lord. The name of the person who, I'm suggesting, threatened her husband. If your lordship agrees, I'll write it on a piece of paper as I don't think it would be fair to bandy it about in open court at this stage.'

The judge nodded. 'I agree. I never approve of persons unconnected with a case receiving possibly damaging publicity as a result of their names being heedlessly introduced into a trial.' He swivelled round to face the jury. 'Members of the jury, you've heard what I've just said. You will, of course, be shown the piece of paper bearing the name after the witness has answered counsel's question.'

The usher, who was hovering beside Mr Orkell, took a folded slip of paper from him and carried it over to the witness.

'Does that name mean anything to you, Mrs Fulmer?'

'It's the name of the man my husband mentioned.'

'The man who was threatening him?'

'Yes.'

'Let me see it, please,' the judge said.

A few seconds later, it was passed to the jury and then to the clerk of the court.

Putting out a hand, Robin Mendip murmured, 'My turn.'

Finally, the piece of paper came to rest before Nick. 'Harry Everett,' he read.

'Know anything about him?' Mendip asked.

'No, but I soon will,' Nick said, making a note of the names, which, he reckoned, would almost certainly be found in the Criminal Record Office register.

Mr Orkell was, meanwhile, continuing his cross-examination. 'Had your husband defended that man on a robbery charge?'

'I believe that's correct.'

'Was it one of those pay-roll hold-ups and was about £10,000 involved?'

'So I understand.'

'And was the man whose name is on that slip of paper acquitted?'

'Yes.'

'And was it some time after that your husband was threatened by him?'

'Yes.'

'Do you know what the cause of their quarrel was?'

'Mr Orkell,' the judge broke in sharply. 'There must be a limit to the amount of hearsay evidence which even the defence may elicit. I think you have had sufficient latitude and I don't see how the witness can possibly answer that question without it being completely hearsay.'

'If it's any help, my lord, I can't answer it at all, because I don't know.'

Gathering his gown around him, Mr Orkell announced that he had no further questions to ask and sat down with an air of satisfaction.

Robin Mendip said that he didn't wish to re-examine the witness and would next call Mr Neil Penfold.

Penfold entered the box with an expression of frowning self-importance, which was increased when he put on a pair of heavy, horn-rimmed spectacles before taking the oath, afterwards returning them to his breast pocket, from which they jutted out in readiness for their next call to service.

Clare had already summed him up as one of those people whose need of spectacles was more tactical than optical. She had seen Nick hurry from the court as soon as Mrs Fulmer completed her evidence and guessed that he had gone to check on the name on the slip of paper. Clare had been fascinated observing Brenda Fulmer in the witness box. Of one thing she felt sure : widowhood was merely a temporary phase in her life.

Moreover, Clare doubted whether the loss of her husband had been much more than a hiccup in her daily routine. She was obviously a tough, self-assured woman of the world who had probably married her considerably older husband for his money, of which, according to Nick, there had been no shortage. This was not surprising seeing that Fulmer and Co. had the sort of clients who were ready to pay large sums of ready cash for the services they required.

Clive Donig had also proved an interesting study. He scarcely took his eyes off Mrs Fulmer while she was in the box and yet never a flicker of emotion was registered on his own face. He might have been a carved figure sitting in the dock. There was something frightening about his lack of expression. Occasionally, he would blink his eyes, but was otherwise immobile, it seemed.

Obviously trying to suppress his urge to fidget, Penfold stood facing Robin Mendip, his brow still gathered in a heavy frown.

After conceding that his full name was Neil Imbertson Penfold and that he lived in Chelsea and was a solicitor to the Supreme Court, Mendip went on :

'How long have you been a partner in Fulmer and Co.?'

'I have been with the firm for six years and have been a partner for three.'

'Were there any other partners apart from Mr Fulmer and yourself?'

'No,' Penfold replied, with a slight start as though someone had caught him naked in the bathroom.

'Did you know anything about Mr Fulmer's visit to Medina Towers on January the eighth?'

'Nothing.'

'He hadn't told you he was going there?'

'Definitely not.'

'Does the firm have any clients living in Medina Towers?'

Penfold moistened his lips. 'Not as far as I'm aware, but I should point out that Mr Fulmer and I had our own areas of work and didn't know everything the other was engaged in.'

'Yes, I follow,' Mendip murmured tactfully, 'but I take it you have checked the firm's records which would show clients' addresses?'

'It's been done.'

'You mean by a clerk, rather than by yourself?'

'Precisely.'

'And you have no record of any client living in Medina Towers?'

'Correct.'

'Are you able to help the court at all as to what Mr Fulmer was doing at Medina Towers that evening?'

'It's a complete mystery to me.'

'Is the accused, Clive Donig, a client of your firm?'

'No.'

'Have you ever seen him before?'

The witness slowly turned his head to look at the man in the dock, who had been staring at him with unwavering intensity. It seemed to Clare that it had almost required a magnet to draw his attention to Donig.

'I have never seen him before in my life.'

Mr Orkell, who was short and rotund and who always found movement in the confined space of counsel's seats an effort, now struggled to his feet not unlike a chick easing its way out of the egg. Penfold watched the purposeful but unhurried activity with apparent anxiety, constantly patting his jacket pockets, pulling out his spectacles and then putting them away again.

Finally upright and peering at the witness over the top of his half-glasses, Mr Orkell fired his opening salvo.

'Would it be correct to say, Mr Penfold, that your firm has, over the years, represented a large number of hardened criminals?'

'I don't understand what you mean by hardened, sir.'

'You don't?' counsel echoed in a calculated tone of surprise. 'Let me explain, then. I mean criminals with records of conviction which show them to any reasonable person to be hardened in their life of crime.'

Penfold gulped. 'We've certainly represented clients who've had the misfortune to fall foul of the law,' he said stiffly.

'Come, come, Mr Penfold, you know perfectly well what I mean. We're not talking about those caught shop-lifting or importuning in doorways. I'm referring to the big-time boys, to use the colloquialism.'

'I suppose we have represented our share of those,' Penfold conceded, nervously.

'I won't quibble about whether you've had your share, but you've had a considerable number of such clients, have you not?'

'I don't have any statistics . . .'

'Mr Penfold, you're fencing with me again,' counsel remarked sternly.

'I'm not denying that my firm has represented people in that category.'

'Many of them dangerous criminals?'

'What do you mean by dangerous, sir?'

'Men who don't hesitate to carry and use firearms. That's what I mean, Mr Penfold.'

'We've certainly represented clients who've been charged with armed robbery. So have a lot of other firms.'

'I'm not asking about other firms. I'm interested only in Fulmer and Co.,' Mr Orkell remarked, fixing the witness with a severe look. He turned to the clerk of the court. 'I'd like the witness to be shown the piece of paper with the name on it that I showed Mrs Fulmer.'

The usher took it from the clerk and passed it to Penfold who had put on his spectacles in anticipation.

'You see that name?' Mr Orkell said.

'Yes.'

'Is it the name of someone who is a client of your firm?'

'Was,' Penfold said quickly, clearly pleased to have an opportunity of putting defending counsel right.

'Thank you. Was.'

'He was Mr Fulmer's client, not mine,' Penfold added hastily.

'I'm grateful to you for making that clear, too,' counsel said, benignly. 'Was he someone acquitted of a charge of armed robbery?'

'Yes.'

'A robbery involving £10,000?'

'Something of that order.'

'When *was* this?' the judge broke in.

'As far as I recall, about eighteen months ago, my lord,'

Penfold replied, apparently grateful for a crumb of judicial recognition.

'And after his acquittal, did this person and Mr Fulmer fall out?' Mr Orkell asked.

'I suppose you could put it that way.'

'How else would you care to put it, Mr Penfold?'

'I gather there was some sort of dispute between them.'

'Relating to what?'

'I can't tell you. I don't know.'

'At all events, did it result in the person issuing threats against Mr Fulmer?'

'Yes.'

'What sort of threats?'

'Threats to get even, whatever he meant by that.'

'How do you know this?' the judge enquired.

'Mr Fulmer showed me a letter he'd received.'

'You have it still?'

'It appears to have been mislaid, my lord. It can't be found. I've looked through Mr Fulmer's case papers without success.'

'What exactly did this letter say?' Mr Orkell asked, after Mr Justice Finderson had bent back over his notebook with a faint, but meaningful, sniff.

'I don't recall it very clearly. There were just threats.'

'Did you read it as a threat to kill, coming from the source it did?'

'I must make it plain that I had never met the client, so it's difficult to answer your question.'

'Have a try!'

'It might have meant anything from a threat to kill to something much less.'

'Were the police informed?'

'That was a matter for Mr Fulmer.'

'Were they informed?'

'I gather not.'

'Why not?' the judge asked with such suddenness that the witness flinched.

'I imagine, my lord, that Mr Fulmer didn't take it all that seriously. If it had been my decision, I would have reported it to the police.'

'It is possible that reporting it might have caused embarrassment to Mr Fulmer?' Mr Orkell asked keenly.

'I'm afraid I don't follow you, sir.'

'Because Mr Fulmer had something to hide in his dealings with that particular client?'

'I know absolutely nothing of any such possibility,' Penfold replied in tight-lipped reproof.

'Very well,' Mr Orkell said, 'I won't press that any further. Now I'd like you to look at another name which I have written on a slip of paper.'

Once more, the piece of paper did the rounds, ending up under Nick's nose.

'George Blaney,' he read, with a frown. Wasn't Blaney one of the Peterson gang who collected a hundred years between them for a series of armed robberies? It'd been about a year ago and the trial had resulted in a great deal of extremely dirty in-fighting, he recalled having heard from an officer concerned with the case.

'Is that the name of a one-time client?' Mr Orkell asked.

'Yes.'

'One of Mr Fulmer's clients?'

'Yes.'

'Is he at present serving twenty years in Parkhurst Prison?'

'I know he received a heavy sentence, but I certainly have no knowledge of what prison he's in.'

'If you please,' Mr Orkell said in his smoothest forensic tone. 'Did he also prove to be a disgruntled client?'

'I can't tell you, though I don't suppose he was very happy with his sentence.'

'Probably not. Do you know that he's a man with a grievance against your late partner?'

'I do not. Though it wouldn't surprise me. Clients such as he frequently bear grievances when things go wrong.'

'What went wrong in his case?'

'When I say, things go wrong, I mean when they get convicted,' Penfold said in a slightly flustered tone.

Mr Orkell nodded in an abstracted manner.

'Do you know where that person's wife lives, Mr Penfold?'

'I've no idea.'

'Has she not had contact with your firm since her husband's conviction?'

'Not with me.'

'With Mr Fulmer?'

'It's possible, but not to my knowledge.'

'Do you not know that the lady in question lives in Medina Towers?'

While a ripple of excitement went round the court, Nick burrowed furiously into his file of papers. Somewhere he had a list of the names of every resident in the three blocks. He was sure that there was no one of the name of Blaney. He found the list and scanned it urgently. There was definitely no one of that name living in Medina Towers. He turned and whispered to Robin Mendip.

Mr Orkell, who had been observing the activity, now glanced at prosecuting counsel who gave him a thumbs down sign. He frowned and bent forward to speak to his instructing solicitor.

Addressing the judge, he said, 'I understand, my lord, that she may have changed her name since her husband's imprisonment.'

Mr Justice Finderson turned to the witness. 'Perhaps we might now hear your answer to the question?'

Penfold smiled weakly. 'I'm terribly sorry, my lord, but I can't remember what the question was.'

'Do you know that the wife of the person whose name you have on that piece of paper lives in Medina Towers?'

'I do not.'

'Either under that name or any assumed name?'

'I have no knowledge of where she is living under any name.'

'There, for the moment, we will leave the mystery, members of the jury, and resume at five minutes past two.' Mr Justice Finderson's tone was frigidly neutral. As he rose to leave court for the lunch adjournment, he said to counsel at large, 'I hope that steps will be taken to resolve it. Either the lady does live in Medina Towers or she does not.'

CHAPTER THREE

'You've got a busy time ahead of you, Mr Attwell,' Robin Mendip remarked as he prepared to leave court.

Nick nodded. 'I hope I may have found out something about Harry Everett by the time we come back. D.C. Cambridge was phoning the Yard straightaway. It may take a bit longer to trace Mrs Blaney.'

'Her name's Ella, if that's any help,' Mendip said with the smile of one happy to spring a surprise.

'How do you know that, sir?' Nick asked in a puzzled tone. Mendip nodded toward his junior, Tom Parrod.

'I prosecuted in the Peterson case,' Parrod said. 'George Blaney was one of five accused. He called his wife as a witness to support what proved to be a completely botched alibi. I happen to remember her name was Ella.'

'Do you also remember where the Blaneys were living then, sir?'

'Hackney, I think. The whole gang came from that district.'

'Not Medina Towers?'

'No, the name would have rung a bell when I came across it in this case. If she does now live in Medina Towers under another name, I assume she moved away and changed her name for the sake of her children. I seem to remember they had a couple of kids of school age.'

'You don't know anything about Blaney's grievance with his solicitor?'

'No; I've been thinking hard since his name cropped up this morning. I recall that Stanley Fulmer represented the younger Peterson, who was acquitted – he was the only accused who did get off – and I suppose Blaney must also have been his client. You know how it is – or rather was – in these cases; you were never quite sure how many clients Fulmer did have in the dock.'

36

'Well, I'd better get busy on the phone,' Nick said, after a thoughtful pause.

He looked round for Clare and saw that she was hovering by the door.

'It's been like old times,' she said with a smile as he came up.

'It's certainly not been a boring morning,' Nick said. 'I wish you could stay on.'

'I must get back to pick up Simon. But before I depart, tell me the name on the second piece of paper.'

'George Blaney. Wife's name, Ella, I've just learnt.'

'Do you have the list of residents of Medina Towers?' Nick nodded. 'May I glance at it a moment?'

Nick extracted it from his file of papers. 'There's definitely no Blaney on it, however you care to spell it.'

Clare studied the list with a furrowed brow. 'What about Mrs E. Bishop of Flat 14 in the North Block?' she said, glancing up suddenly.

'Go on.'

'E. Bishop. E. Blaney. Same initials. I've often noticed that people like to stick to their initials even though they alter their names. One can understand it. After all, it minimises the confusion. Anyway, it's a long shot which might be worth investigation. You've got to begin somewhere, so why not with Mrs E. Bishop?'

Nick gave her a fond look. 'You're a clever girl and the cleverest thing I ever did was to marry you. I'll see you this evening, though heaven knows when. It'll probably be quite late.' He gave her a quick kiss.

He wouldn't have done that in the main hall of the Old Bailey a few years ago, Clare reflected with gratification as she turned to leave.

Nick was about to go in search of D.C. Cambridge when he suddenly materialised at his side.

'Sorry, but I'm a bit out of breath,' Ted Cambridge said, 'I've just run up four flights and down again.'

'Stairs always separate the sheep from the goats,' Nick replied unkindly. 'It's lucky you don't have to be really fit to play that game of yours.'

'Not much you don't,' Ted Cambridge replied indignantly. He took his hockey extremely seriously and the one sure way of getting a rise out of him was to suggest that it wasn't a truly manly sport. 'Do you realise, Nick . . .'

'Tell me what you've been able to find out about Harry Everett,' Nick interrupted, before the other could assail him with some of his well rehearsed facts and figures about the game.

Ted Cambridge took a deep breath. 'He has a list of convictions longer than your arm. Mostly for dishonesty, but three for crimes of violence, including armed robbery. However, he hasn't been in trouble since he was acquitted at this court in September of the year before last. It was an armed pay-roll hold-up and it would seem that the jury accepted his alibi. Ten and a half thousand pounds was the haul, not a penny of which was ever recovered.'

'Anyone else charged with him?'

'No, it was a one man job. I gather he's always been a loner.'

'Where'd you find this out, Ted?'

'From ex-Detective Inspector Walsh. It was almost his last case before retirement. I managed to track him down at the headquarters of Wonder Foods, where he's security officer. They run a chain of supermarkets in the Epsom area. He remembers the case well and says there wasn't any doubt that Everett was the right man, but that Stanley Fulmer fitted him up with an alibi which the jury swallowed.'

'Does Walsh know anything about the subsequent quarrel between Everett and Fulmer?'

Ted Cambridge nodded keenly. 'He says there was a strong underworld rumour that Everett entrusted the money to his solicitor, who, when the time came, didn't hand back the full amount.'

'Fulmer chiselled him?' Nick said, with a grin.

'Well and truly, if the rumours were anything to go by. But Mr Walsh says they were never substantiated and Everett was certainly in no position to shed his tears in front of the police.'

'Nor was Stanley Fulmer likely to have reported the threats to anyone. Did Walsh know about the threats, too?'

'No. He heard that Everett was hopping mad and merely says that he wasn't the sort of person to take things lying down. He regards him as one of the nastiest criminals he ever came across.'

'We'd better bring ourselves up to date on Harry Everett,' Nick observed.

'I've found out where he's living,' Ted Cambridge said. 'It's an address in Hammersmith.'

'You've unearthed a lot in a short time, Ted. Well done.'

Nick went on to tell his side-kick about Blaney, whose name had cropped up in the trial after Ted Cambridge had gone off on his enquiry about Everett.

'We'll have to try and see both Everett and Ella Blaney this evening. You can do some preliminary work this afternoon weeding out the residents of Medina Towers who definitely can't be Ella Blaney. That should considerably reduce the list of people to call on.'

'Mrs E. Bishop certainly sounds a hopeful.' Ted Cambridge frowned thoughtfully. 'I covered most of the flats in the North Block and I'm almost sure I called at Flat 14. I'm trying to think . . . Yes, I remember Mrs Bishop. She was a small, blonde woman in her thirties. She became uptight when I said I was a police officer; but that went for a fair number of the residents of Medina Towers. The police are not their favourite visitors. And I also remember now that there was a kid flitting about in the background while I was talking to her at the door. She knew about the murder, of course; they all did. She just gave the standard reply that she couldn't help the police with any information and the victim was unknown to her.'

'Well, we'll try and jerk her memory,' Nick said. 'Provided she is Ella Blaney.'

'Who'll we see first?'

'Everett. But before then, I've got a date with Gordy.'

'Have the defence tried to find out where our information came from?'

'Not yet. I don't know whether Mr Orkell will have a go at me when I'm in the box.'

'The judge should shut him up if he does. Protection of police informers is still a recognised principle, though the way things are going, it probably won't be long before they are thrown to the wolves with the rest of us.'

'Thrown to the wolves is about right,' Nick observed. 'The only reason the defence ever want to find out is so that he can be taught a lesson when it's all over. That and to neutralise him as a future informer.'

As soon as he had golloped a sandwich and a cup of coffee, Nick hurried back to court. Neil Penfold was hovering outside and made to speak to him, but Nick held up a hand.

'You mustn't talk to me, Mr Penfold. Not while you're still giving evidence.'

Penfold looked faintly flushed and Nick reckoned that he had been drinking. After the drubbing he'd had, it was understandable, if incautious.

Robin Mendip had already returned to his seat and Nick told him what had been found out about Harry Everett and of the further action he was proposing to take.

'That sounds fine,' Mendip remarked.

'Has Mr Orkell told you what line the defence is going to take, sir?' Nick asked.

Mendip shook his head. 'I wouldn't have thought there was any defence on the facts. I suppose it's just possible the jury'll accept that the money really did represent gambling winnings, though they'll have to be pretty gullible. But I don't see how he can explain away his possession of the revolver.' Mendip lifted his wig and scratched the top of his head. 'My bet is that they're going to dig out all the evidence they can to show that there are dark, sinister figures in the background, on whom the real responsibility lies.'

'But that doesn't let Donig out.'

'Of course, it doesn't. But it's only by pleading not guilty that the defence can get the whole story on record.'

'You should have quite a field day, sir, when you come to cross-examine Donig.'

'*If* he goes into the box.'

'You mean, he mayn't give evidence?'

Mendip shrugged. 'I think it's a distinct possibility.'

'But then he's bound to be convicted.'

'He's bound to be, anyway, provided our firearms witness doesn't suddenly stand on his head.'

'I thought Donig might suggest that the gun was planted on him.'

'He may as a forlorn hope.' Mendip pulled out his handkerchief and began to clean his spectacles, holding them up to the light to judge the success of his handiwork. 'Assuming we're right about this being a contract murder, do you imagine there was an intermediary – or possibly more than one – between Donig and the contractor?'

'I'd have thought it was quite likely there was a middle man, sir.'

Mendip nodded. 'So that Donig may genuinely not know who wanted Fulmer put down.'

'That wouldn't worry him, sir. Provided the money was all right, he'd do the job.'

'I noted that he has a conviction for manslaughter a few years back. I presume that wasn't a contract killing?'

'It was a fight outside a pub. A much smaller man was viciously beaten up and died from his injuries. Donig's defence was that the man had attacked him first and that he only acted in self-defence. There was also rather confused medical evidence as to the exact nature of the dead man's injuries and the subsequent cause of his death. All in all, it was enough to reduce a possible charge of murder to manslaughter and to get Donig a suspended sentence from a soft-hearted judge.'

Mendip smiled. 'An unoriginal story right to its end,' he observed.

A few seconds later, Mr Justice Finderson returned to court and Neil Penfold resumed his place in the witness box.

Robin Mendip rose. 'Before my learned friend continues his cross-examination, my lord, perhaps I might just inform your lordship that the police will, as a matter of urgency, be enquiring into the matter of the lady who may or may not live in Medina Towers. They will also be making some enquiries about the other name introduced into evidence by my learned friend; the person who was said to have made threats against Mr Fulmer.'

'Thank you, Mr Mendip. I'm sure the officer will realise that a certain amount of delicacy will be required in the circumstances.'

Mr Orkell came to his feet with the grace of a plumpish animal squeezing through a narrow aperture.

'If I may be so bold as to endorse what your lordship has just said about delicacy. It would be most unfortunate if police action were in any way to embarrass the defence.'

The judge looked at defending counsel with a quizzical expression, but made no comment.

Nick reflected sardonically that they'd all wiped their hands in advance of any muck-up he might make of his enquiries and reserved their right to be wise after the event. However, there was nothing new in that so far as the police were concerned.

Mr Orkell thrust his head forward and glared at the witness who gave the impression of bracing himself for further martyrdom.

'Would you agree, Mr Penfold, that you have been unnecessarily obstructive in this case?'

'Certainly not.' Penfold cast a rapid glance at the judge as if expecting him to blow a whistle and declare a foul. But Mr Justice Finderson refused to be drawn.

'My instructing solicitors were in touch with you on several occasions before the trial seeking your assistance, is that not so?' Mr Orkell went on.

'Yes, they did get in touch with me.'

'Seeking your assistance?'

'They wanted access to information, which I had no right to give them.'

'Why not?'

'It was information relating to clients of my firm and I'd have been in breach of privilege in disclosing it.'

'Is it not true that you advanced this claim of privilege because there were matters you wished to conceal; matters which reflected adversely on Mr Fulmer?'

'That's a monstrous suggestion.'

'But is it a true one?'

'It most certainly is not.'

'Were you any more forthcoming to the police?'

'I don't take your meaning, sir.'

'I'd have thought it was fairly clear. Did you also refuse the police access to information about your clients?'

'Yes; for the same reason.'

'Or was it, in each case, in order to hide a scandal?'

Penfold turned toward the judge and in an emotional voice said, 'My lord, I seek your protection against this outrageous attack on my firm's integrity.'

'As I understand Mr Orkell's questions,' the judge said in a matter-of-fact tone, 'it's not so much your firm's as your late partner's integrity which is being impugned.'

'That's quite right, my lord,' defending counsel observed. 'My only accusation against Mr Penfold is that he has behaved misguidedly in not being more frank with the defence or with the police.'

'Yes, well we have his answer to that and I suggest you move on to another topic.'

'I have no further questions to ask the witness, my lord.'

'You wish to re-examine, Mr Mendip?' the judge enquired, peering down at prosecuting counsel.

As one counsel sat down and the other stood up, Neil Penfold ran through a gamut of fidgets.

'The suggestion has been made, Mr Penfold,' Mendip said in a slight drawl, 'that if you had thrown open your office files, both the defence and the police would have been greatly assisted in this case. Have you any reason to believe that to be so?'

'No, sir.'

'Was it purely professional privilege and not any attempt to conceal a scandal that motivated you?'

'It was, sir.'

'Do you have in your possession any evidence, other than that which you have given, which might help resolve some of the unexplained features surrounding Mr Fulmer's death?'

'None, sir.'

'Thank you,' Mendip said and sat down. Turning to his junior, he whispered, 'I felt I had to go through those motions. After all, he is our witness!'

Tom Parrod nodded and smiled. He personally had some sympathy with the hapless Penfold, who had been left to bear the burden of his senior partner's sins and who had been placed in a most invidious position by Stanley Fulmer's dramatic death.

Penfold had made to leave the witness box when the judge stopped him.

'Just one moment, Mr Penfold, I have one or two questions I should like to ask you and I anticipate that the jury will find it helpful to have your answers.'

Penfold appeared to freeze and then reluctantly retrace the couple of steps he had taken toward departure.

'Of course, my lord,' he said nervously.

'Did Mr Fulmer keep a desk diary?' Mr Justice Finderson enquired mildly.

'Yes, my lord.'

'Generally speaking, was it a satisfactory record of his appointments?'

'Yes.'

'Including his social engagements?'

'He wouldn't put in the full details, my lord. For example, if he was going to the theatre, he might just put, "7.30, Apollo Theatre", without giving the name of the play.'

'That sounds eminently reasonable. Now tell me this. What was the last entry for January the eighth?'

'Four forty-five, Mrs Smith, my lord.'

'Mrs Smith being a client?'

'Yes.'

'Supposing he had recorded his proposed visit to Medina Towers, what entry would you have expected to find?'

'Either "Medina Towers" with a time, or possibly the name of someone with a time.'

'Or even both?'

'Yes.'

'Are you, of your own knowledge, aware of any outside appointment kept by Mr Fulmer which was not recorded in his desk diary?'

'My lord, I wasn't given to inspecting his desk diary,' Penfold said with a wail.

'I'm sure you weren't, but you might still be able to answer my question.'

'My lord, I'm only surmising, but I would not be surprised if there weren't a number of Mr Fulmer's appointments which, for one reason or another, never got recorded.'

'When you say "for one reason or another", do you have in mind forgetfulness or wilfulness?'

'It might be that a client turned up without an appointment and he was able to see him and didn't enter it in his diary after the event.'

'But that wouldn't be the case with his visit to Medina Towers?'

'No, my lord, I agree. Of course, it could be that he only decided to go there after he'd left the office that evening.'

'The fact he had told his wife not to expect him home until nine o'clock doesn't seem to sustain that theory,' the judge observed mildly. 'Tell me this, does it surprise you that Mr Fulmer kept this seemingly mysterious appointment in Medina Towers without a single known person being aware of what he had in mind?'

Penfold shifted uncomfortably. 'Not really, my lord. Some of our . . . his clients made rather a fetish of secrecy.'

'Hmm! What size staff do you employ?'

'Eight in all.'

'Quite small.'

'Yes, my lord.'

'With you and your late senior partner the only two qualified lawyers in the firm?'

'Yes.'

'I imagine you must have frequently discussed matters together?'

'When it was necessary, my lord.'

'Were your offices close together?'

'Quite close.'

'How close?'

'Next door to one another actually, my lord.'

'With a connecting door by any chance?'

'No,' the witness replied, with obvious relief at being able, at least, to deny that intimacy.

'Well, thank you, Mr Penfold. Do you wish to be released?'

'I should be most grateful, my lord.'

'Any objection, Mr Mendip? Mr Orkell?'

'I imagine the witness will be available to come back if required?' Mr Orkell remarked.

Both counsel and the judge looked toward Penfold, who was nodding energetically. 'I can return within half an hour, my lord, if I'm wanted.'

'Very well, then,' Mr Justice Finderson said briskly, 'you may depart.'

As Penfold made his way out of court, the young clerk

45

representing the Director of Public Prosecutions Department leaned across to Nick and murmured with relish, 'I reckon he had his tail so twisted that it'll never be straight again.'

Nick grinned back and nodded. He had been observing the jury again. They looked a better bunch than he had first thought and had seemed particularly interested and attentive when the judge had been asking his questions. Even the egregious Trevor Lee's mask of general contempt had, to a certain extent, faded.

It didn't mean that an approach might not still be made to suborn one of them, but it did render it less likely to succeed. And that, reflected Nick, was more than half the battle.

CHAPTER FOUR

The remainder of the afternoon passed off without further drama. The next four witnesses testified to hearing shots fired or running feet, and to the action each of them subsequently took.

Mr Orkell amused himself by emphasising the vagaries of human observation and recollection. One witness, under cross-examination, described the sound of the shot as being akin to a loud pop, while the next said it was like the time her television set blew up and a third said it was more like a cannon going off.

All four told the court of what they saw when they looked out of their respective windows. But here again it was difficult to credit that each had witnessed the same thing, namely Stanley Fulmer slumped beside the driver's door of his car.

The one witness who had heard someone running from the scene was led into such a flight of fancy that the judge had to call for quiet when smiles turned into ripples of laughter. The unfortunate witness in question was left to goggle at the reaction he had occasioned. But as Robin Mendip said afterwards, if you will describe running feet as sounding like the flapping of bats' wings in hell, what can you expect?

When, at a quarter past four, the court adjourned, Mendip wished Nick good luck in his evening's enquiries and said he would be at court at half past nine the next morning to hear their result.

While Nick was gathering up his papers, D.C. Cambridge pushed his way into court against the exiting throng.

'I've made a list of twenty-three flats where Mrs Blaney may be living,' he said, sitting on the edge of the table which filled the well of the court.

'What's your criterion?' Nick asked.

'Where there's no male in the household. Of course if she's

taken a boy-friend on board while her husband's out of circulation, it's too bad. For us, I mean.'

'O.K., Ted, we'll meet at the Yard just before eight o'clock. If I'd known how things were going to turn out, I'd have arranged to meet Gordy earlier, but I can't alter that now.'

When Nick arrived at his rendezvous with Gordy a few minutes early, it was to find his informer already there. He was sitting at the same table they had occupied the previous evening with a mug of tea and a cheese and pickle sandwich in front of him.

'Go and get yourself something, sarge,' Gordy said graciously, waving toward the counter. 'By the way, this lot's not been paid for,' he added, in case Nick had been given the wrong impression.

Nick returned to the table with a cup of tea for himself. It couldn't be more foul than the coffee. He could tell from Gordy's expression that he had not been able to find out much and was wondering how he might still squeeze some money out of Nick. He looked more shifty than usual.

'Well?' Nick said.

Gordy shook his head sorrowfully. 'I haven't stopped working for you, sarge, since we parted outside 'ere last night.'

'What have you found out?'

'Them two blokes I over'eard talking. They 'aven't been back. But I've been keeping my ears open, sarge.'

'And?'

'I can't 'elp remembering it's only 'cos of me you got on to Donig.'

'That debt's been paid,' Nick said. 'You know what the rules are, payment by results. To-night you're empty-handed.'

'I'm entitled to something, sarge.'

'I've paid for your tea and sandwich.'

Gordy's sense of outrage at this callous remark was such that he actually choked in the act of swallowing. When he pulled out a grubby handkerchief, a number of £5 notes came, too. Nick refrained from comment, but admired the speed with which Gordy palmed them out of sight.

'I been reading about the case in the evening paper,' he said, as if sensing that a change of subject might be desirable. 'Going all right, is it?'

'So far.'

'Nobody trying to find out 'ow you got on to Donig?'

'No. And if they do, they won't get anywhere. You're quite safe.'

Gordy looked about him with a furtive air.

'I run a lot of risks for you, sarge.'

'So you keep on reminding me.'

'I reckon you'll get promotion after this case, thanks to me.'

'I'll buy you another sandwich if that happens.'

Gordy's mind was obviously elsewhere, because after a thoughtful pause he asked, ' 'Ow's Donig looking?'

'He doesn't show any emotion at all,' Nick replied and went on, 'I've asked you this before, but who do you think he suspects as having grassed on him?'

'One of the blokes what gave 'im the contract. 'Oo else?'

'I'm surprised you've not been able to come up with something on that.'

'Come off it, sarge, I'm not God Almighty.'

'If he thinks it was someone connected with the contract, he must have an idea who.'

' 'E may think it was a bird. Birds can turn nasty and spiteful and Donig 'ad a fair number.'

'None we've been able to trace.'

'They was probably avoiding you, sarge.'

'But you got it from a chap in the pub?'

' 'Sright. From Charlie 'oo'd 'eard it from a bloke just out of stir.'

'What'd you tell me Charlie's other name was?'

Gordy looked aggrieved. 'Honest, I don't know, sarge. I just knew 'im as Charlie. 'E came from Liverpool and said 'e was going back there. That's why I 'aven't seen 'im since. I told you all that.'

Nick ignored the reproach. Gordy always assumed an air of injured innocence when he thought Nick was trying to catch him out.

'Ever heard of George Blaney?' Nick asked.

' 'E's doing twenty years on the island, in't 'e?'

'That's right. What can you tell me about him?'

'Nothink, sarge, why are you interested?'

'I just am. What about Harry Everett, know anything about him?'

' 'Arry Everett?' Gordy said with a judicious air. 'I seem to know 'is name. What's it worth, sarge?'

'Depends what you can tell me about him. He was once a client of Fulmer's.'

' 'Oo 'asn't been a client of Fulmer's?'

'You, or so you told me.'

'It's true. I never was one of 'is. A firm out Wembley way looked after me last two times. That was before I started going straight,' he added with a touch of pride.

Nick regarded Gordy as about as straight as a country lane. 'We'll meet here again to-morrow evening, Gordy. Perhaps you'll have a bit more to tell me by then. To-day hasn't been worth the bus fare.'

'If I didn't respect you, sarge, I'd give up.'

Not while there's any money to be had, you wouldn't, Nick reflected. The trouble with informers like Gordy Warren was that you could never be sure how many irons they had in other people's fires. Convention forbade one police officer poaching another's informer, but there was still wide opportunity for duplicity. Hence the strict rules governing the use of informers and their payment.

Gordy had certainly proved his worth to Nick, but their relationship, from Nick's point of view, was rather like a marriage of convenience to a whore.

They parted company outside the café and Nick stood for a moment watching his informer scuttle off down the street, swathed in his over-long raincoat. He moved rather like an insect with a strong wind behind it, giving the impression at times of being blown irresistibly forward.

Ted Cambridge was waiting in the car out of sight in a nearby street, having suggested that this would save a bit of time.

'He's not been able to find out anything about the jury nobbling,' Nick said flatly as he got in beside his companion.

'With luck we shan't have any trouble after the judge's warning to the jury to be on their guard.'

The street that Harry Everett lived in appeared to have little to commend it apart from uniformity. Two rows of early

Victorian semi-detacheds faced each other. A light shone through the glass panel above the front-door of number 48.

Ted Cambridge pressed the bell and then rapped on the door with his knuckles. The man who opened it looked almost as unpromising as his C.R.O. photograph, which they had taken an opportunity to look at.

'Mr Everett?' Nick said.

The man said nothing, but just stared at them. He was thick-set and wearing a red sweater which was zipped up to the neck, an old pair of slacks and, on his feet, slippers which had long since lost their shape. He had dark hair slicked back from a straight line across his forehead and sticking out spikily at the back. He had a small, thin mouth from one end of which a matchstick protruded.

'I'm Detective Sergeant Attwell,' Nick went on, 'and this is Detective Constable Cambridge. We're both from Scotland Yard.'

'What d'you want?' Everett asked, almost without opening his mouth. The matchstick, however, managed to end up on the other side.

'We'd like to talk to you.'

'What about?'

'It'd be easier if we could come in.'

'What d'you want to talk about?' Everett demanded, without moving.

'About Stanley Fulmer's death.'

'I don't know nothing about it.'

'But you knew him?'

'So'd a lot of other people. Go and talk to them.'

'Your name's come up in the course of the trial.'

'My name?' Everett said, viciously spitting out the matchstick.

'That's right. If you want to hear more, you'd better let us in.'

Standing aside, he nodded at a door just on the right of the hall. 'That room.'

It was almost bare of furniture and obviously seldom used from its appearance and musty smell.

Harry Everett followed them in, closed the door and leaned against it.

'What's this about my name coming up?'

'I gather Fulmer defended you on a robbery charge about eighteen months ago.'

'I didn't do it. The jury said so.'

'Did you have a row with Fulmer after the case?'

'Who says so?'

'I'm asking you.'

'And I'm not answering any questions until I know more.'

'The rumour is that Fulmer cheated you out of some of the money and you threatened to get even with him. Is that true?'

Everett gave a mirthless laugh. 'How could he have cheated me when I didn't do it?'

'Because the jury acquitted you doesn't mean you didn't do it.'

'Oh, that's the police for you! Doesn't matter how many juries say you didn't do it, they go on saying you did. Is it surprising everyone hates their guts?'

Nick turned to Ted Cambridge. 'He's not very bright, is he?'

'Dim as a torch with a run-down battery, if you ask me.'

'You can't needle me with that sort of talk.'

'Let's call it quits then.'

'Who mentioned my name?'

'The defence.'

'Donig's mouthpiece?'

'That's right. He wrote it on a bit of paper, so the press haven't got hold of it.'

Everett frowned. 'So what's he mentioned it for?'

'As someone who had a grudge against Fulmer and might have wanted to kill him.'

'But Donig did that.'

'Nobody believes that Donig did it off his own bat. He was a hired killer.'

'You mean there was a contract out for Fulmer?'

'Exactly. Were you the contractor?'

'Don't be daft. You'll die of old age before you can prove anything as daft as that.'

'You still haven't said whether or not you had a row with Fulmer after your acquittal.'

'And I'm still not saying, because it's nobody's bloody business. What I am telling you is that I didn't have nothing to do with his death.'

'Any ideas as to who did?'

'You've got someone, what more do you want?'

'I've told you that.'

'Well, you can go and knock on someone else's door. I'm not shooting my mouth to the police. There's too many doing that, as it is.'

There was a brief silence; then, gazing around the room, Nick asked, 'Live here alone?'

'Since my missus upped and left me, yes,' Everett said with a note of defiance.

'Where d'you work?'

'That's my business. I'm not having the police poking their noses in there.'

'I can probably find out easily enough.'

'Find out, then. But if you start making trouble for me, I'll start making it for you.'

Nick glanced at his companion. 'Ready to go, Ted?'

D.C. Cambridge nodded. 'We may want to see you again, Harry,' he said. 'Depends on what sort of course Donig's trial takes.'

Everett opened the door and walked ahead of them to open the front one.

' 'Night, Harry,' the two officers said in turn as they left, but Everett just glowered.

'Unattractive bit of goods,' Nick remarked as they went across to their car.

'Wonder why his wife left him? Not that she could have found it difficult to find someone better.'

'Anyway, one interesting thing emerged. Did you notice that he was the first to mention Donig's name?'

Ted Cambridge nodded. 'Yes, it struck me, too.'

'He's obviously fairly alive to the case and we'll have to make it our business to probe a bit further. We must try and find out who his associates are.'

'Mr Walsh did say he'd always been a loner.'

'I know, but no criminal can operate entirely in a vacuum. Not all the time.'

'We can try and find out if his name has ever been linked with Donig's.'

Nick nodded thoughtfully. 'The trouble there is that, if it was Everett who put Donig up to the murder, I don't see why Donig should be bandying his name around. After all, it must have been Donig who gave Everett's and Blaney's names to his counsel. Unless, of course, there was an intermediary in the deal who acted for Everett.'

'It's a bit of a puzzle, I agree. Intermediary or not, someone gave Donig his instructions and he must surely know who it was. And yet he's not let drop a dicky-bird.'

'Sooner or later, he will. It mayn't be until after he's been convicted, but he'll say something then. I can't believe he'll go off to serve a life sentence, still saying nothing.'

'Particularly as he must suspect whoever it is as being the person who shopped him.'

Nick glanced at his watch. 'We should be at Medina Towers by half past nine. Any thoughts on how we tackle Mrs Bishop?'

'If we call her Mrs Blaney as soon as she opens the door, we mayn't even get inside.'

'That'd apply whether she was or wasn't. I think it'll have to be the soft approach.'

Twenty minutes later Medina Towers hove into view, its three high-rise blocks silhouetted against London's lit-up sky. Ted Cambridge was about to bring the car to a halt when Nick said, 'Not here, drive on a bit.'

'If you say so, but what's wrong with there?'

'It's where Stanley Fulmer parked his car.'

'Not superstitious, are you?'

'No, but it's a bit like walking over someone's grave. I don't, unless there's no alternative.'

Ted Cambridge drove on a further twenty-five yards and pulled up. A few minutes later, they stepped out of the lift on the fourth floor of the North Block.

'Number fourteen's round on the right,' Ted Cambridge said.

'Glad I don't live in a place like this,' Nick muttered, as they turned along the open balcony which was swept by a chill breeze. 'Crazy construction having all the front doors open out round the perimeter.'

'It's an Arab design. Hence Medina Towers.'

'Who wants an Arab designed block of flats in the East End of London where the wind comes straight from the North Sea?'

They arrived outside Number 14 and Ted Cambridge pressed the bell. They heard a door inside being opened and then footsteps approaching the front door.

'Who is it?' a female voice called out.

'Is that Mrs Bishop?' Nick asked.

'Yes, what do you want?'

'Can you open the door and I'll explain.'

It was opened a few inches to the limit of the chain and a face appeared. It was a sharp face surmounted by short, fair hair that resembled a close-fitting cap.

'Who are you?'

'We're police officers. May we come in?'

'What do you want?'

'Just to talk to you for a few minutes. We can't carry on a conversation through a crack of the door. Moreover, I see one of your neighbours already peering round the edge of a curtain.' Nick had used his most persuasive and reasonable tone and was rewarded by the chain being slipped off and the door opened to admit them.

After closing the door, the woman led the way into the living-room where a boy of twelve was sitting on a stool in front of a television set. He looked up and stared gravely at the visitors.

'You'd better go to bed, Ricky,' the woman said. 'These two gents want to talk.'

'Sorry if we've interrupted a good programme,' Nick said to the boy, who merely turned and left the room.

'He didn't hear you,' the woman said, 'he was born deaf.'

It was then Nick realised that there was no sound coming from the set. Only the picture was showing.

'But he understood you,' Nick said with interest.

'He can lip-read me. He's very bright for his age and considering his handicap.'

'Does he go to a special school?'

The woman nodded. 'They've done wonders with him.' She

glanced at Ted Cambridge and frowned. 'Aren't you the one who called a few months ago after that murder in the street outside?'

'You've got a good memory for faces, Mrs Bishop.'

'I don't remember every face I see,' she said without expression, leaving her visitors to divine such meaning as they could.

Nick looked around the room. 'Apart from Ricky, are you alone?' he asked.

'My daughter's out. She's fifteen.'

'And your husband?'

'He's away.'

Nick bit his lip in thought. Contrary to expectations, he found he rather liked Mrs Bishop. She had a certain dignity and the deaf Ricky had touched him. He knew how he would have felt if Simon had been born with some physical defect; worse still, with a mental abnormality. Of course, if she didn't prove to be Mrs Blaney, his feelings did not matter. But he felt more than ever certain that she was George Blaney's wife, defiantly coping while her husband lived out his middle years in prison.

'Mrs Bishop,' he said gently, 'are you sure you told the truth when Detective Constable Cambridge came to see you about the murder?'

Her mouth quivered slightly. 'I don't know what you mean,' she replied in a voice scarcely above a whisper.

'You denied any knowledge of Stanley Fulmer, the man who was shot. But you did know him, didn't you?'

'Why do you say that?' she asked, as if realising she was being irresistibly drawn toward a cliff's edge.

'Isn't your real name Mrs Blaney?'

She closed her eyes and put out a hand to steady herself. When she opened them again, Nick found himself looking into a face whose expression was one of bleak despair. She seemed unable to speak, but he now knew for certain the answer to his question.

'Mrs Blaney, I realise something of how you must feel,' he went on, 'and I promise I won't do anything to aggravate your anguish if I can help it, but I must know the truth. Did Stanley Fulmer come to see you on the night he was killed?'

It was at that moment that they all heard a key turning in

the front-door and a few seconds later a girl shot into the room. She paused in surprise when she saw the two officers and threw her mother a questioning look.

She had a healthy outdoor look about her and gave the impression of having just run all the way home for the fun of it. Her short curly hair had a wind-blown look and her face was flushed with youthful excitement.

'We won, Mum,' she said, when nobody spoke.

'Sylvia's in her school gymnastics team,' her mother said in an abstracted tone.

The girl gave her mother a worried look. 'Is everything all right, Mum? Who are these . . . these men?'

'They were just about to leave,' Mrs Blaney said, as if she had reached a sudden decision.

'We had almost finished talking to your mother, Sylvia,' Nick said. 'Could you leave us for a few moments?'

'Stay in the room, I don't want you to go,' Mrs Blaney said in a quick, anxious tone.

Nick sighed. 'You do realise that we'll have to come back. Isn't it better we should finish our conversation this evening rather than return? For your own sake as much as anyone's.'

Sylvia's moment of return couldn't have been less fortunate, for Nick was sure that, but for her entry, Mrs Blaney would have talked. He felt that she was torn by a desire, on the one hand, to confide in someone and, on the other, a determination not to say anything which might imperil her new fragile security.

In Flat 14 in the North Block of Medina Towers she was Mrs Bishop doing her best to bring up two children, one of them handicapped, the family's immediate past buried in a grave, albeit an all too shallow grave.

Nick felt genuinely sorry for the woman, if irked by the abrupt turn their visit had taken. He gave her a final hopeful look, but she refused to meet his eyes. As far as she was concerned, their visit had already ended. Nick gave a shrug and moved toward the door.

'Will you see them out, Sylvia?' her mother said in a tense voice.

The girl went out into the hall and Nick motioned Ted Cambridge to follow her. Then he turned back into the room and went over to where Mrs Blaney was standing in a pose of frozen misery.

'I really do understand how you must feel, Mrs Blaney. I realise, too, that you regard the police with a certain amount of suspicion. Assuming you had nothing to do with Fulmer's death, I really will do my best not to make things worse for you. On the other hand, I shall continue nagging until you do talk. I'm convinced that Fulmer did call on you that evening and I must know why. I don't want to embarrass you by turning up again in my heavy boots at your front door, because I realise what gossipy people there are in a block like this. And two police officers knocking on doors is bound to excite comment.' He gave her a smile. 'The fact is that even plain clothes officers usually seem to look the part, so I'm going to arrange for someone who is not a police officer to come and see you. She's not from the Town Hall either. She's my wife and she normally stays at home and minds the kid. What you say to her will be off the record. O.K., she'll tell me, but it can't in any way be used as evidence in that form or be held against you. So think about it. She'll come about ten o'clock tomorrow morning. If you're not here or you refuse to talk to her, then I'll have to come back myself and your chances of maintaining a low profile and keeping the neighbours from gossiping will be considerably less.' He became aware of Sylvia standing in the doorway. 'Yes, I'm just coming.'

He was lost in thought as he and Ted Cambridge waited for the lift. He had seldom nailed his colours to the mast quite so strongly. He knew he had taken a risk in putting his trust so firmly in the woman. If he was proved wrong, he'd really be bawled out for having stepped so far out of line. But police work was compounded of risks. If you never departed from the rule book, you'd end your days as a back-room pen-pusher. Of course, if you departed from it too far and came unstuck, you were at least as likely to end up the same way.

'Must be hell trying to keep a home going when your husband's tucked up in prison for years to come,' Ted Cambridge remarked as they stepped into the lift and he pressed the button for descent.

'What was Fulmer doing, visiting her that evening? Assuming he did.'

'My theory is that he was having it off with her and that one of her husband's friends decided to teach him a lesson on George's behalf and, at the same time, to warn Ella to behave herself.'

'Killing someone is more than teaching them a lesson.'

'Well, it'd have been a lesson to her.'

'If you're right, one presumes it wasn't Fulmer's first visit there.'

'Probably eight o'clock every Thursday night as regular as clockwork. Those sort of arrangements usually are.'

'I wonder.'

'What's your theory, Nick?'

'I don't have one. I don't know why he went there. But I'm going to find out.'

'What are you planning to do about her?'

'I'm not sure.'

D.C. Cambridge threw his sergeant a faintly exasperated look. 'Personally, I'm not sure we wouldn't have done better to have shoved the girl out of the room and put the pressure on her mother. It didn't need much more to break her down.'

'Do you think she may have set the whole thing up herself?'

'What, lured Fulmer to her flat and arranged for him to be shot as he left?'

'Yes, something like that.'

Ted Cambridge stuck out his lower lip and thought for a moment.

'A bit like crapping on your doorstep, isn't it?'

'Not when you consider it has taken us several months to find out whom he was visiting.'

'I suppose it's a possibility and yet I don't see her as that sort of person.'

Nick nodded. 'Then that's something we're agreed on. I don't either.'

Ted Cambridge grinned. 'Your trouble is that you're a romantic, Nick. Just because you and Clare are happily married and faithful to each other and because Ella Blaney struck a sympathetic chord with her plucky little mother role, you don't want to believe that she'd have it off with another man, even though she may have to wait a dozen years or more before she has George back in her bed.'

'Poppycock!'

When they arrived outside the Attwells' house in Barnes, Nick invited Ted in for a nightcap.

'No thanks, Nick, or I'll be late for a date. But give my love to Clare.'

Ted Cambridge had the reputation of being free and easy with his favours and, certainly, he never seemed to be short of girl-friends. The ones Nick had met were attractive, too. But then, he was quite a good-looking young man in an ordinary sort of way and his unflagging energy was probably as much of an asset in the more carnal of his pursuits, as it was on the hockey field.

Clare was watching television, but came running out into the hall as Nick opened the front door.

'Hello, darling,' she said, kissing him warmly. 'I'm so glad you're back. Your dinner's in the oven. You haven't eaten, have you?'

Nick shook his head. 'A cup of tea with Gordy has been my only refreshment since midday. Ted and I have been on the trot the whole evening. He's just dropped me off.'

'Why didn't you ask him in?'

'I did, but he has a date.'

'Did you call on Mrs Bishop?' Clare asked eagerly. Nick nodded. 'And was she . . . ?'

Nick pulled her toward him and kissed her once more, this time for longer. Then he said, 'That's the answer. Now lead me to my dinner and I'll tell you the rest.'

As he ate, he brought Clare up to date on everything that had happened since her departure from court at lunchtime. When he related what had happened on their visit to Mrs Bishop, who was almost certainly Mrs Blaney, and what he wanted Clare to do, she stared at him with a mixture of dismay, incredulity and interest.

'But, darling, how could I go and see her to-morrow, anyway? I've got to collect Simon and Alexander from play-school and bring them back here for lunch.'

'You don't have to collect them until half past twelve and

I've arranged for you to be at Medina Towers at ten. You can take the car.'

'I should think that's just about the slowest way of getting across London in the morning rush hour.'

'Then go by Tube. There's a station only five minutes' walk from Medina Towers. The whole journey can't take more than an hour, which'll give you an hour and a half with Mrs B.' Noticing her expression, Nick said contritely, 'I'm afraid I had forgotten that Alexander was coming to-morrow. I was thinking you'd be able to ask Sally to pick up Simon.'

'She did that to-day,' Clare said.

'Yes, I remember now. If it's any help, I'll drop Simon at play-school in the morning, so that needn't hold you up.'

'You'll have to give him and yourself breakfast, too. I'll need to be away by half past eight.'

Nick realised that he was not in a strong position to argue the toss about times and he refrained from pointing out that they'd always breakfasted by half past eight, anyway. Simon usually needed a bit of chivvying, but Nick himself seldom took more than three minutes to eat a plate of cereal, followed by a slice of toast. His cup of coffee was drunk in the act of pushing back his chair and standing up.

'I'm sure she'll open up to someone sympathetic like you, darling. She's longing to talk to somebody; I could feel it.'

'And supposing she confesses to having had a part in Fulmer's murder, what do I do then?' Clare asked. 'It really could turn out to be a very tricky situation, Nick.'

'I know it *could*, but I don't believe it will. I don't think I've misjudged her and if I haven't, then she wasn't involved in his death.'

'Supposing Ted's theory proves correct, what are you going to do then?'

'If she was having an affair with Fulmer, that's not criminal.'

'No, but it's highly relevant in the context of Donig's trial. You couldn't just suppress that information and allow the case to take what you knew to be a false turning.'

'I've got to know whether or not Fulmer did visit her and, if so, for what purpose. Not until I know the answer, can I decide what to do with the information. I'll almost certainly have to tell Mr Mendip . . .'

'And he'll have to tell the defence.'

'But I still believe I can protect her, provided she has not done anything criminal.'

'Supposing she has to go to court, how can you protect her then, Nick? The press'll be on to her in no time and the poor woman will have to re-make her life all over again, if she has the necessary spirit.'

'I'm backing a hunch, Clare, and there are bound to be risks, but I still feel they are worth taking.'

'You realise that you're putting your career in her hands to a certain degree? Supposing she reports my visit to the police or talks to the press, what'll you say?'

'I've thought of all that,' Nick said stubbornly. 'Indeed, I'd thought of it all before I ever mentioned it to her. She may be married to a crook, but I believe she's a straight and honest woman coping as best she can.'

'It'll be a joke if, after all this, she turns out not to be Mrs Blaney,' Clare remarked with a smile.

But Nick remained serious. 'She is Mrs Blaney and if anyone can get her to talk it'll be you.'

Clare sighed. Her misgivings were centred on the repercussions her role might have on Nick's career if his superiors ever came to hear of it. But then she thought of the employment of all the unorthodox means she had heard about in the course of her own service and she also remembered her own unofficial part in several of Nick's cases. The short answer lay in whether such means brought success. Everything was judged by success. But in the present instance it was success which was going to lead to possible embarrassment and worse.

She glanced at Nick who wore a worried expression as he sipped a steaming mug of tea.

'What's on your mind?' she asked.

'That maybe I *was* wrong to have involved you. It seemed such an obvious idea when I was there. But now I'm less sure.' He gave her a rueful look. 'I sometimes forget that you're not still W.P.C. Reynolds.'

'As long as you don't ever forget that I'm primarily Mrs Nick Attwell, I don't mind,' Clare said, coming round the table to where he was sitting and kissing the top of his head.

CHAPTER FIVE

As she sat watching her husband eating his asparagus, Olive Tishman decided, not for the first time, that it was one of life's less agreeable sights. It wasn't just the rivulets of melted butter on his chin, but the concentrated energy with which he tackled each stalk, munching his way from one end to the other until only a few fibrous strands were left.

They were sitting opposite one another in a small, expensive French restaurant in the West End after a visit to the theatre.

Although it had been warmly recommended by some friends, neither of them had liked the play and had said so in an exchange of grunted comments during the interval and after the final curtain.

A waiter arrived at their table but departed again when he saw that Frank Tishman had not yet finished his asparagus. His wife had long since daintily disposed of a small grapefruit. As her next course was to be filet de boeuf en croûte, she had decided to go easy on the first. It was a pity that her husband had not shown similar restraint, she reflected, as she gazed at his still handsome, but increasingly fleshy, face.

At last the final piece of asparagus was gone and he mopped his chin and sluiced his fingers in the small bowl of warm water beside his plate. Then picking up his glass, he took a noisy gulp of wine, leaving two greasy lip marks behind. After this, he glanced at his wife.

'You're very silent this evening.'

'I could say the same about you.'

'I've been busy eating. Asparagus requires all one's attention.'

'So I observed.'

'Meaning what?'

'That eating it seemed to be a full-time occupation.'

'One of us might as well try and enjoy the meal. It's costing enough.' He paused. 'How did it go in court to-day? I've not had time to look at an evening paper.'

'It went all right, I think.'

'Brenda didn't find it too much of an ordeal?'

'I don't think so.'

'What about Penfold?'

'He didn't seem too happy giving evidence.'

'I'm not surprised. Fulmer and Co. have a fairly unsavoury reputation in the law. Stanley must have left quite a few skeletons rattling in the firm's cupboards.'

With a brittle smile, Olive Tishman said, 'And there are none at all in yours?'

Her husband looked at her sharply. 'We weren't talking about me. If you're to become successful in business – and I have been – you inevitably have to take the occasional risk. You also inevitably make enemies. Little people who are envious of one's success and get spiteful.' He picked up his wine glass which the waiter had just re-filled. 'We wouldn't eat in places like this and live in Mayfair if I hadn't made a packet. And you can't make a packet without cutting a few corners and treading on any feet that get in the way.'

'Aren't you ever afraid?' she asked, still in a needling sort of tone.

'Afraid of what?'

'Oh, forget it . . . it doesn't matter.'

Her husband cut off a piece of steak and examined it on the end of the fork. Then swivelling round, he called out to the maître d' who was standing a few feet away.

'Look at it, Tino! I asked for very rare, this looks as if it's been under the grill since yesterday teatime.'

Tino tut-tutted and swept up the plate of offending steak. 'I'm so sorry, Mr Tishman, I will order another immediately.' He turned to Olive Tishman. 'And yours, madam, is it all right?'

'Perfectly delicious,' she said, smiling at him sweetly. In a confiding tone, she added, 'I know just how difficult it is to cook a steak to my husband's taste.'

'I hope that made you feel better,' Frank Tishman said after Tino had departed to the kitchen.

'I don't follow you.'

'Trying to make me appear difficult in front of Tino.'

She gave a mirthless laugh. 'I didn't have to do a thing.'

'What's wrong with you to-night?' he asked, irritably.

'Wrong? Nothing's wrong with *me*.'

'Then for heaven's sake, stop behaving like a bitch.'

Her cheeks coloured. 'So that's what I am now, is it?'

'I didn't say that. I merely said you were behaving like one at the moment.'

'I don't suppose you've ever called Brenda a bitch.'

'I've never had occasion to; nor a whole lot of other women. But why drag in Brenda's name?' he asked suspiciously.

'Brenda told me to-day that, shortly before his death, Stanley had accused her of having an affair with you.'

'Ah! So that's what's made you behave in this way.'

'So you admit it?'

'I do nothing of the sort. It's quite untrue. Didn't Brenda tell you the same thing?'

'I don't necessarily believe everything my sister tells me.'

'She'd hardly have mentioned it, if it were true. Hasn't that occurred to you?'

'I'm still puzzled why she did tell me. I can only think it was something to do with the influence of being at court and reliving part of Stanley's life.'

'You mean she just came out with it quite suddenly?'

'It was while we were having lunch and she was talking about Stanley and said with that tantalising little smile of hers, "Do you know, Olive, Stanley actually thought I was having an affair with Frank? He said as much not long before he died." '

'And what did you say?'

'I was so flabbergasted, I didn't say anything for a time. Then I asked her if it was true and she said, of course not.'

'So now you have it from two sources that it's not true.'

'And are you saying that Brenda never told you?'

'Did she say that she had?'

'You don't want to be caught out giving the wrong answer, do you?'

'You needn't take that line. I've got nothing to be caught out over. The answer is that Brenda has told me nothing. This evening's the first I knew of the whole silly suggestion.'

'Silly? Is that what you call being unfaithful to your wife? Except it's rather more than that. I mean going to bed with your sister-in-law is a rather specialised taste. But I suppose you'd justify it as keeping it within the family.'

'You know as well as I do that your sister has never been beyond a bit of mischief-making. And she's certainly excelled herself on this occasion. If there's truth anywhere in the story at all, it can only be in Stanley's belief that Brenda was being unfaithful to him. We only have Brenda's word that he ever did accuse her; but *if* he did and *if* he named me, he was wildly off course. Mind you, I wouldn't blame Brenda. Stanley was fifteen years older than she and not every girl's cup of tea, even if she did marry him. Though as we've always known, it was never exactly a love match.'

'Of course you're only eight years older than Brenda.'

With exaggerated patience, Frank Tishman laid down his knife and fork beside his newly-arrived steak.

'I'm getting the bill,' he said curtly. 'If you want dessert, you can stay and eat it by yourself, because I'm leaving.'

They sat silent in opposite corners of the taxi which took them home and as soon as it pulled up outside their block of flats, Olive Tishman stalked in ahead of her husband.

He hurried after her and just managed to squeeze between the closing lift doors while her finger was still on the button.

'Bitch,' he said angrily, slapping her hard across the face. 'You're lucky I didn't do that in the restaurant and humiliate you the way you tried to humiliate me.'

Their front door was directly opposite the lift, so that no one saw them get out and enter their flat. Olive Tishman went immediately to the bathroom and locked herself in. Her husband got himself a large brandy and tossed it down in one. Then, after a few seconds' thought, he left the flat, slamming the front door hard behind him so that his wife should hear his departure.

He was still simmering with anger when, ten minutes later, the taxi drew up outside the address he had given to the driver.

It was not the first time the Tishmans had had a row, nor the first time he had struck her; nor even the first time he had stormed out and left her alone all night.

For a while she sat with her feet up on the sofa, drink in

hand. Her cheek still smarted and she wondered whether she would be able to show herself the next day. It wasn't like a black eye which could be explained in a variety of ways. This mark was red, with red tentacles, one for each finger.

After about forty minutes, she reached for the telephone and dialled a number. She could hear music in the background when the receiver was lifted.

'Am I disturbing you, Brenda?' she asked. 'You haven't got anyone with you?'

Her sister gave a soft laugh. Olive could tell that a hand was placed over the mouthpiece as clearly as if she were in the room and witnessed it. Then Brenda's voice spoke.

'No, you're not disturbing me at all.'

'I only rang for a chat. We saw such a dreadful play this evening.' With this topic quickly exhausted, she said, 'Have you decided whether you're going back to court to-morrow?'

'Yes, I've said I'll be there. But there's no need for you to come, as I'm not expecting to be recalled into the witness box and so shan't need your moral support. I'm just going as a spectator.'

Shortly afterwards they bade each other good night and rang off.

Normally, Brenda would have said, 'Give my love to Frank,' before ringing off. But to-night she hadn't done so.

There could be only one explanation, Olive reflected bitterly. Frank was there to receive it in person.

CHAPTER SIX

Crenly Street had a seedy and, at the same time, buoyant air. Its buoyancy was provided by the colourful, small shop-keepers who fought a tenacious rearguard action against the authorities seeking to tear down the decrepit buildings and replace them with faceless offices and a multi-storey carpark. The shop-keepers were, for the most part, foreigners; Italians, Cypriots and others of Mediterranean origin.

The street's seediness was reflected in the peeling façades which lined it and in the down-at-heel appearance of many who thronged it.

Anyone seen looking anxiously about him, endeavouring to spot the haphazardly placed numbers of the various premises, was usually a client of Fulmer and Co. making a first visit to the firm's offices which lay above a delicatessen, reached by a narrow staircase at the side of the shop.

Neil Penfold had never liked their accommodation, but Stanley Fulmer had always argued that Crenly Street put their clients at ease and gave them a sense of reassurance. They could slip in and out without attracting anyone's attention, which was an important consideration. With a sly smile he would also point out that the fire escape at the back, which led down into an alleyway and from there into a parallel street, was a convenient feature. If any particularly sensitive client was worried that he had been seen by unfriendly eyes to enter, he could always slip away unnoticed. Penfold had often reflected in more carefree moments that, if they were allowed to issue a brochure extolling their services, these features would be prominently mentioned.

But it was in no carefree mood that he arrived at the office on the morning after his Old Bailey appearance. He was nagged by doubt and worry.

Percy, the firm's senior clerk and, perhaps, the person who had worked closest with Stanley Fulmer, had been out at court when Penfold returned from the Old Bailey the previous after-noon, so he had not yet heard the junior partner's account of his ordeal.

However, not long after Penfold had sat down at his desk the next morning, there was a quiet knock on his door and Percy came in. He was a small man with a round face and a bald head, who could be bonhomous or vindictive according to his assessment of the circumstances. Those who had thought he was always the cheerful extrovert were apt to be quickly disillusioned. He had been with the firm for thirty years and had, in the eyes of many, led a charmed life. To be Stanley Fulmer's chief clerk and stay out of trouble required a special brand of toughness and resilience.

' 'Morning, Neil,' he said. 'Sorry I wasn't around when you got back yesterday, but I had a bit of trouble to sort out at Inner London and then I went on to Brixton to see a couple of clients who want bail.'

When they were alone, he always addressed Penfold by his first name, but was punctilious about calling him Mr Penfold in the presence of others.

'You've seen the papers this morning?' Penfold enquired.

'Only the *Mail*, which gave a fairly factual account. I gather Orkell probed around a bit.'

'He was like a dentist determined to find a cavity.'

'And he touched a few sensitive spots, eh?'

'It was inevitable. Nobody believes Donig was on his own. In fact, Mendip opened it as being a contract murder with person or persons unknown in the background. I don't see why it has to be that. Just because the police have not been able to discover a link between Donig and Mr Fulmer doesn't exclude the possibility that one existed.'

'I don't believe Donig had any reason to kill S.F. on his own initiative. Whatever you say about the possibility of a link, I've not been able to find one. I've made a fair number of enquiries as I've gone around, largely to satisfy my personal curiosity, and I've discovered nothing. I'm sure the police are right. It was a contract murder.'

Penfold was silent for a while. Then meeting Percy's watchful gaze, he said, 'You knew Mr Fulmer's clients better than I did, Percy, which of them would you consider capable of having put out the contract?'

'And had the motive to do so, you mean?' Percy replied with a thoughtful air.

'Naturally.'

'You see, there are quite a few who wouldn't feel sentimental about having someone knocked off, but there aren't many with the motive so far as S.F. was concerned.'

'Who?'

'Most of them, of course, are inside, which cramps their style. Not much you can do when you're in the security wing at Parkhurst or Leicester. You generally have to wait until you're out before you start planning something of that sort. At least, you can *plan* it all right while staring at your cell ceiling, but that's about all.'

'Anyone not inside who had motive and will?'

'The only one who springs to mind is our old friend, Harry Everett.'

'His was one of the names the defence put to me.'

'I'm not surprised. He and S.F. fell out really badly after his last case.'

'Did Mr Fulmer really cheat him out of some of the proceeds, do you think?'

Percy gave a throaty chuckle. 'No good asking me things like that, Neil, I wouldn't know. There were certain deals that S.F. played very close to his chest. My thoughts on the matter are no better than your own. But the fact remains that Harry Everett did, as we both know, threaten S.F. after the case and it was enough to make S.F. hire a bodyguard for a while. I told him I thought it was a waste of money, but I suppose it gave him a bit of extra confidence. But if someone like Harry Everett is out to kill, he isn't going to be deterred by the hiring of a bodyguard. He'll just revise his planning.'

'What's our latest information on Everett?' Penfold asked after a pause.

'He's still living in the same house in Hammersmith. His wife left him a few months ago. He has a job in a junk yard, sorting the stuff out. Rumour has it that he's in the market to be propositioned.'

'What's his speciality?'

'He was an all-rounder. Could turn his hand to anything. He was never frightened of a bit of rough stuff, which made him useful in certain types of job.'

'My understanding is that he operated on his own. He wasn't a member of any gang.'

'Latterly, he was a loner, but he's worked with a number of different gangs in his time. His trouble is that he's a difficult cuss and he invariably quarrelled with the people he worked with and they didn't want to see him again. But he hasn't really got the equipment to be a successful loner.'

'He got off on his last job,' Penfold observed.

'Thanks to S.F. If Everett had been brighter, he wouldn't have been caught by the police in the first place.'

'So you think he may have set this whole thing up? That it was he who hired Donig?'

'All I'm saying, Neil, is that he had motive and will . . .' His voice trailed away and Penfold looked at him with a puzzled expression. He could tell that there was something further on the clerk's mind, but he knew better than to try and prod him.

After a pause in which Percy seemed to be weighing up pros and cons, he made a sudden decisive sound and went on, 'As a matter of fact, I picked up an interesting bit of information from one of the clients I saw at Brixton Prison yesterday evening. He knew that Donig's trial had started and asked what I thought the outcome would be. But his chief interest was who had put out the contract. I asked him if he had any ideas on the subject and he shook his head. But a moment or two later he said the only person Donig had ever got on with was Harry Everett. They'd worked together on some job a few years back and none of the others liked either of them, but they hit it off with each other.'

Penfold let out a low whistle. 'That's most interesting.'

'I thought you'd find it so.'

And yet Penfold felt certain that Percy had nearly not told him. He wondered what motive the clerk might have had for keeping it to himself.

'Did our client know whether they'd been around together recently?' he asked.

'No. He didn't move in either of their circles and this was

just something he mentioned in passing. It came out à propos Donig's reputation for being generally feared in the underworld. He's regarded as a bit mad. Well, he's obviously a psychopath of some sort. Hired killers, mercenaries, they all are.'

'Did our Brixton client know of Everett's quarrel with Mr Fulmer?'

'Apparently not.'

'Which makes his mention of Everett the more significant.'

'Yes.'

Penfold stared in frowning concentration at the top of his stained and pitted desk, while Percy watched him with the faint smile of a bored parent waiting for his child to finish his homework.

'I'd like to go through the Everett file again.'

Percy nodded. 'I'll fetch it.'

'It's all right, I'll ask Betty to get it from the cabinet.'

'As a matter of fact, it's on my desk. I've just been through it myself. Perhaps you'll find it more illuminating than I did.'

He got up and left the room, returning two minutes later and dropping a fat, buff-coloured folder on Penfold's desk. At the top of the folder, there was written in untidy capital letters, 'In Re Harry Everett'.

'I must get along to Knightsbridge Crown Court,' Percy said, glancing at his watch. 'I'll be back by early afternoon.' He reached the door and paused. 'There are still quite a few things we ought to discuss, Neil. Time may be shorter than we think.'

'What do you mean by that?' Penfold asked sharply.

'The future of the firm. I know I'm only a clerk, but I have been here much longer than anyone else and I'd like to know what you have in mind.'

'But what do you mean about time being possibly shorter than we think?'

'Once this trial is over, and depending on what else emerges, I think we must expect to come under someone's microscope. We ought to adjust our thinking to that prospect.'

'I see what you mean.'

'It'd be a pity if all the goodwill S.F. built up were to be washed down the drain. Anyway, I must be off. We can discuss the whole scene when you've had time to ponder it, Neil.'

After Percy had gone, Penfold continued staring at the door. When his secretary entered bearing a cup of tea, she gave a start.

'What's the matter, Betty?' he asked when he became aware of her watching him, the cup still in her hand.

'You had such a funny expression on your face, Mr Penfold.'

'Oh, did I?'

He managed to give a short laugh, though he was feeling anything but amused.

CHAPTER SEVEN

Clare spent her whole journey trying to decide her exact approach to Mrs Bishop/Blaney at the moment when she opened the front door and they came face to face.

But she was no nearer a decision when she turned a corner and saw the three blocks of Medina Towers ahead of her framed against a grey, unpromising sky.

A number of children were playing in the open space surrounding the block and she narrowly missed being struck by a vigorously kicked football. There were also two groups of women with prams and push-chairs gossiping, but no one paid her any attention.

She joined a small boy waiting for the lift. When it arrived he marched in ahead of her and took charge.

'Which floor do you want, miss?'

'Fourth, please.'

She noticed he pushed her button and then the one for the twentieth.

'Do you live right at the top?' she asked in a friendly tone.

He shook his head. 'Sixth. I just go up for the ride and come down. You can come, too, if you want.'

'I think I'll get out at the fourth, but thanks all the same.'

The lift jerked to a halt and Clare stepped out. She rounded a draughty corner and, a moment later, found herself outside the front door of Number 14.

She paused a second before pressing the bell. All she could do was announce herself and hope for the best. She could think of no magic password to make the situation easier.

'I'm Clare Attwell,' she said with a hesitant smile, when the door was opened. 'I believe my husband called on you last night and said I'd come and see you today.'

The woman looked tired and Clare judged that she had not slept much the previous night.

'Is it all right for me to come in?' Clare went on, when the

74

woman just stared at her but said nothing. At least, she hasn't slammed the door in my face, she thought.

The woman gave a helpless shrug and stood aside for Clare to enter. In the living-room she motioned her to a chair and spoke for the first time.

'Would you like a cup of tea? The kettle is boiling.'

'That would be lovely,' Clare said enthusiastically.

The woman went out and returned a couple of minutes later carrying a tray of tea things. Clare noticed there was a small lace cloth on the tray, as well as two cups and saucers, milk jug and sugar bowl. It had clearly been prepared in advance, which must indicate that she had decided to admit Clare before actually seeing her on the doorstep.

'Milk and sugar?' she asked.

'Only milk, please,' Clare said, putting out a hand to receive the cup. After taking an appreciative sip, she set the cup and saucer down on a small table beside her chair. 'Would you prefer I called you Mrs Bishop or Mrs Blaney?' she asked in a sympathetic voice.

'What's it matter, now you know who I am. I'm still George's wife whatever I call myself. I only did it for the children's sake. Everyone at their previous schools knew their father had been sent to prison for twenty years and it just wasn't fair on them so we moved here and I became Mrs Bishop. The welfare people were very helpful.'

Clare nodded. 'It must have been desperately difficult for you and from what my husband told me, you've obviously got two fine children.'

Mrs Blaney nodded. 'They're all right most of the time. Ricky's the problem with his deafness, but he's getting on much better since we moved to this district. Sylvia's at a difficult age for girls, but luckily she's so caught up in her gymnastic classes, it takes up much of her spare time and she doesn't hang around boys the way so many of them do. And some of the boys round here are pretty rough.' She paused and frowned. 'I suppose my talking like that may surprise you, seeing I have a husband in Parkhurst Prison who is considered to be a dangerous criminal.'

'It doesn't surprise me in the very slightest. I'm merely

75

filled with admiration at the way you appear to cope with the difficulties.'

Mrs Blaney shrugged as if to indicate that she had no alternative but to do as she did.

Clare went on, 'I think my husband told you why he came to see you. It's about the trial at the Old Bailey arising out of Stanley Fulmer's death. Up to now, the police have been unable to discover what Fulmer was doing in this area when he was shot. As you know, they made door to door enquiries in Medina Towers, but no one was able to help. Of course, at that time they had you recorded as Mrs Bishop and didn't know you were George Blaney's wife. Then at the trial yesterday, the defending barrister produced a bit of paper with your husband's name written on it and asked Fulmer's partner Penfold, who was giving evidence, if he knew the name, and if he also knew that Mrs Blaney was now living in Medina Towers. So you see it all came out through the defence.'

Mrs Blaney nodded. 'Once one person knows, it isn't long before others do. An associate of George's discovered we'd moved here and I suppose the word went around.'

'And that really brings us to the crunch question, Mrs Blaney, did Fulmer call and see you that night? Is that why he was in this area?'

The woman gave a little shudder and stared at the cup and saucer held between her hands. Looking up, she said, 'What'll happen if I talk to you?'

It was the very question Clare had hoped to avoid being asked, but now it had come and an answer was required. Moreover, she realised that everything hinged on the answer she gave. She might have thought she was asking the crunch question, but now she had got one back.

'Mrs Blaney, I'm reluctant to believe you had anything to do with Fulmer's death. If I'm right, then the worst that could happen from your point of view is that you might have to go to the Old Bailey and give evidence.' She noticed the look of alarm on the woman's face and hurried on, 'But if you did have to go to court, I'm sure it could be arranged that your new identity could be kept secret and you might be able to write your address on a piece of paper which only the judge would see. That happens quite often when a witness has an acceptably good reason for not disclosing her address in open court.' Clare paused. 'But if you were in some way involved in Fulmer's death, I don't think you ought to talk to me any further. I'm certainly not here to hear any confessions of that nature and I don't wish to.'

'I had nothing to do with his death,' she said flatly and Clare let out a sigh. 'It's true he came to see me that evening, but I had no idea what was going to happen when he left. When I heard that he'd been shot, I was scared stiff and when the police came round knocking on doors, I denied any knowledge of him because I realised by then that they didn't know he'd been here. I knew I'd had nothing to do with his death, so I lied out of self-protection. If I hadn't, there'd have been questions and visits to the police station and more questions until the whole of Medina Towers knew everything about me.' Her hands began to tremble and the cup rattled violently against the saucer, so that she put it on the floor beside her. 'I just couldn't face going through that all over again,' she said in a voice of despair.

'If it's any comfort, I'm pretty sure I'd have reacted in exactly the same way,' Clare said, and meant it. 'Are you willing to tell me why he visited you?' she added after a pause.

Mrs Blaney's expression told her that she was re-living events that were past and yet still fresh in her mind.

'George should never have gone down. The case against him wasn't strong and Mr Fulmer thought he had a good chance of getting off. That is, he did at the beginning. Then something happened. George suspected that Fulmer was got at, that he was advised to pull his punches by someone who didn't want to see George acquitted. The result was that some of the stuff George gave his solicitor never reached his barrister and was never put before the jury. After the trial was over, I saw Mr Fulmer outside the court and I told him I shouldn't rest until I'd managed to ditch him in the way he'd ditched George. I told him he wasn't fit to be a lawyer and wouldn't be for much longer if I could help it.' She sighed heavily. 'I did write to the Home Office and the Public Prosecutor's Department and to the Law Society, but you know how it is. They all write back sympathetically either saying it's none of their business or they can't do anything without proof. But I did keep on at the Law Society, because they're the people who're meant to do something about solicitors who behave like Fulmer. Anyway, I suppose Fulmer got to know or had a guilty conscience or something, because early in January he phoned and said he'd like to visit me as I'd got the whole thing wrong and I was being unfair to him. Well, I knew I wasn't being unfair and that he'd shopped George deliberately, so I told him I didn't want to see him. But he went on and on and said he was sure he could persuade me I was wrong about him and surely I wouldn't refuse to see him. So in the end, I said he could come if he wanted, but that it'd be a wasted journey. It was about three days later, I've forgotten the date, that he came. It was around eight o'clock in the evening. He began a long explanation of how it wasn't his fault that George's defence hadn't been successful, but I cut him short and told him I wasn't interested and didn't wish to hear any more and would he leave. When he said he'd come a long way to see me, I said that was his fault as I'd made it clear I hadn't wanted to see him.'

'Were either of your children at home?' Clare broke in.

'They were both out. That's why I agreed to that particular evening. I knew they wouldn't be at home.'

'And when did you know he'd been killed?'

'It was about ten or fifteen minutes after he'd left, I heard police sirens. I went out on the balcony, but couldn't see much. Then one of my neighbours who'd gone down to find out what had happened came and told me that a man had been shot getting into his car. It never occurred to me it was Fulmer. I didn't discover that until the next morning and then I really was in a panic.'

'Did you tell anyone that he was coming to see you?'

'Not a soul. I didn't even mention to the children that I was expecting a visitor that evening.'

'So no one could have learnt from you that he was coming?'

She shook her head vigorously. 'Definitely not. I didn't want him to come and now I wish more than ever that he never had come.' She gave Clare a defiant look. 'His death doesn't move me, it's the trouble he brings into my life that I mind about.'

'Did your husband know about his coming here?'

She shook her head again. 'I haven't told him. He's got enough to worry about without that. I'm able to visit him once a month and the first time I went after Fulmer's death, he talked about it. I won't tell you what he said.'

Clare could imagine that his erstwhile client would scarcely have shown signs of mourning in the circumstances.

'Wasn't he curious that it had happened outside Medina Towers?'

'Yes; and suspicious. But I simply said there was no evidence he'd been visiting anyone here and hundreds of people lived in the neighbourhood. I also pointed out that he had no reason to know I'd moved into Medina Towers and that satisfied George.'

'As a matter of fact, how did Fulmer find out that you lived here?'

'It was my fault. I had a letter from him about two months ago concerning some money George had deposited with him. It was sent to my old address and I collected it from the post office. I'd deliberately not given a forwarding address when we left Hackney. But when I replied to the letter, I gave this address.'

'And the name of Bishop?'

'No. I didn't think Blaney would mean anything to the postman, if I received the odd letter in that name. He'd just assume there was someone of the name staying here. It was stupid of me in a way, though it was the neighbours in Hackney I was running away from more than Fulmer and Co. And I had to reply because I wanted the money.'

'And he sent it to you?'

'Yes. Perhaps he thought it would keep me quiet and that I wouldn't go on denouncing him to the Law Society.'

Clare could think of no honest circumstances in which George Blaney might have deposited money with his solicitor, but decided that this was none of her business, anyway.

The interview had surpassed her hopes and she couldn't wait to tell Nick of its outcome. She glanced at her watch and made to get up.

'I have to get back to the other side of London, Mrs Blaney, to pick up my son and another small boy from play-school. If I don't hurry, I'll find them like orphans on the doorstep.'

'How old is your boy?'

'Three and a bit.'

'George is devoted to our two. It's the hardest part for him not seeing them grow up. And they need a father's influence.'

She threw Clare another faintly defiant look as though she half expected her to reply that a father in prison wasn't fit to be a father at all.

'This is pure nosiness,' Clare said, as they moved toward the door, 'but where do you come from? I can tell that you're not a Londoner.'

'I'm from Bedfordshire. I grew up in a village there and came to London to find a job.'

It all fitted, Clare reflected. Mrs Blaney was obviously an intelligent and quite well educated woman; not one who had grown up in the slummier parts of London and left school at the earliest opportunity. She wondered how she had come to meet George Blaney.

At the door, she thanked her for having been so frank and added that she was sure she wouldn't regret it.

'I hope that you may even feel better for having unbottled yourself,' Clare said, as they shook hands.

It was only while she was travelling home and going over in her mind everything Mrs Blaney had said that something rather unusual occurred to her.

At no time, had the woman said, 'You do believe me, don't you' or anything similar, as so often comes from the lips of those putting on an act and anxious to convince.

Presumably she expected Clare to believe her. And Clare did.

CHAPTER EIGHT

While Mr Orkell pursued his cross-examination of the fire-arms expert, Nick sat wondering how Clare was faring with her visit to Medina Towers. It was lucky, in a sense, that everything had become such a rush that morning, because it had meant there had been no time for further discussion. Simon had been in one of his rare early morning fractious moods, which had delayed his getting washed and dressed and, finally, breakfasted. The air had been thick with recalcitrant noises on the one side and shouts, pleadings and threats on the other. But, eventually, Clare had managed to get away and, soon afterwards, Nick had dumped a sour and grumpy Simon at his play-school. Happily, his friend Alexander had arrived at the same moment and Simon's first smile of the day had broken through.

Having failed to make any impact on the evidence of the firearms expert, Mr Orkell sat down rather sooner than Nick had expected.

The pathologist, who was due to give evidence next, had not yet arrived at court, nor had the laboratory witness who was to follow him.

Under the judge's somewhat displeased gaze, Robin Mendip murmured the necessary apologies and said that, if his learned friend Mr Orkell had no objection, he would call Detective Sergeant Attwell out of sequence.

Mr Orkell replied that he had no objection but would ask to have the right to re-call him at a later stage of the trial should the defence consider it necessary.

The judge then delivered a short homily on the iniquities of wasting a court's time by not having witnesses available at the right moment and on the unfortunate confusion to the jury of hearing evidence out of chronological order.

The regulars in court had heard it all before and listened impassively, while the jury displayed no perceptible reaction, save for Trevor Lee who gave the impression of expecting nothing better.

Nick's own evidence fell into two parts. The arrest of Donig and the finding of the gun and the money in his room was the first aspect and the second concerned the interviews with the accused at the police station. Other officers, mostly uniformed, dealt with the actual scene of the crime and what was found there when they arrived with sirens going and blue lamps flashing only minutes after the shooting had taken place.

Mendip took Nick through his evidence and sat down.

Nick watched Mr Orkell wriggle to his feet and waited. This was the time for maximum concentration. He mustn't allow his mind to wander for a second. He must forget Clare and her mission to Medina Towers.

Some officers professed not to mind cross-examination, but to Nick it was never less than an ordeal. He invariably left the box feeling as though he had just completed the Olympic marathon course.

Mr Orkell peered at him over the top of his half-glasses as if he were studying the label on a dubious bottle of wine.

'Tell me, Sergeant Attwell, is it not somewhat unusual for an officer of the rank of detective sergeant to be put in charge of a murder enquiry?'

'Detective Superintendent Drinn was the actual officer in charge, sir, but he had to go into hospital for a back operation about the time of the Magistrates' Court hearing.'

'And you've been left on your own since then?'

'No, sir. Detective Superintendent Bramber has been supervising the enquiry since then, but most of the investigative work was complete by the time Mr Drinn was taken ill.'

'Hmm, I see. I suppose it must mean that your superiors have a fairly high opinion of your capabilities, eh?'

'That's not for me to answer, sir,' Nick said stonily.

'Perhaps not, perhaps not,' defending counsel murmured, picking up his notebook and bending it right back.

Nick was unsure whether the question had been asked as a form of ingratiation or to trap him into a display of arrogance which could later be turned against him.

'Am I right in thinking that no clues whatsoever were left at the scene which could have led you to the accused?'

'That is correct, sir.'

'Nevertheless, two days later you went to this address in Hackney where you found Mr Donig, a gun and some money?'

'Yes.'

'What took you there?'

'We received certain information, sir.'

'A tip-off?'

'Yes.'

'From an informer?'

'Yes.'

'I'm not asking you for the name of the informer, because I'm sure you won't disclose it, but do you personally know who it was?'

Nick glanced quickly at the judge who laid down his pen and fixed defending counsel with a worried frown.

'You're treading on delicate ground, Mr Orkell. You know, as well as I do, that courts never force police officers to reveal the identity of their informers unless there are exceptional grounds for doing so.'

'But my lord, I thought I'd made it clear, I wasn't asking for his name.'

'I'm aware that you said that. But you're starting to probe and I can't see why, unless it is to identify the officer's informer in a roundabout fashion. I suggest that we hear the officer's answer to your last question and that you then leave the subject.'

'If your lordship pleases,' Mr Orkell said in a tone which repudiated any feeling of pleasure on his own part. 'What is the answer, sergeant?'

'Yes.'

'Yes, what?' counsel asked grumpily.

'Yes, I do know who provided the tip-off.'

'And so on the eleventh of January you went to this address in Hackney and in a ground floor room you found the accused?'

'Yes.'

'He was in bed?'

'He had to get out of bed to let us in.'

'That's not surprising at seven o'clock in the morning, is it?'

'I agree.'

'Was he surprised when you told him who you were?'

'Extremely.'

'Nevertheless he let you in.'

'He didn't have much choice.'

One of the jurors closest to the witness box smiled, but quickly suppressed it when Mr Orkell glowered in his direction.

'The revolver, as you've told the court, was found wrapped in a piece of cloth in a drawer?'

'Yes.'

'What else was in the drawer?'

'Items of clothing. The revolver was at the bottom underneath the clothing.'

'Would it have been possible for someone to have lived in that room without knowing of the existence of the revolver in the drawer?'

'The revolver was well hidden, if that's what you mean, sir.'

'There were no fingerprints on it?'

'That's correct, sir.'

'Will you agree that it could have been planted there without the accused's knowledge?'

'Only by someone having access to his room. There's a lock on the door and the window has a special bolt. The accused never mentioned his room having been broken into. Nor did he suggest the weapon had been planted.'

'I shall be obliged if you will just answer my questions and not regale us with other unsought information,' Mr Orkell said severely. 'The £2000 in notes which you found were in a carrier bag in a cupboard in the room, is that right?'

'Yes, sir. It was a small cupboard at the foot of the bed.'

'Was it locked?'

'No.'

'Why should you doubt that they were winnings from gambling?'

'Because the accused refused to supply us with any details of where and when.'

'You say that he refused, but he said remarkably little at any time, didn't he?'

'I agree he didn't say much.'

'But he denied shooting Mr Fulmer?'

84

'Yes.'

'And you have been quite unable to find any evidence to prove that the accused and Mr Fulmer knew each other?'

'I agree.'

'Hence this fanciful, rather melodramatic, theory that the accused was hired to commit the murder. You agree that it's fanciful and melodramatic?'

'No, sir.'

'But it's the best you can come up with?'

'I'm only concerned with facts, sir.'

Robin Mendip now rose to his feet. 'To be fair to Sergeant Attwell, my lord, he has never testified in the box about it being a contract murder. That was my description when I opened the case to the jury.'

Mr Orkell gave an impatient shrug. 'My learned friend may be strictly correct, but it's quite plain it's the police view that this was a so-called contract murder.' Glancing at Nick, he added, 'That's right, isn't it?'

'Yes.'

'Then let's cease this beating about the bush,' defending counsel remarked crossly and went on, 'Have you had an opportunity of enquiring about those two names I put to Mr Penfold yesterday?'

'Yes, but they are still continuing and I would prefer not to go further at this stage. Certainly I've learnt nothing so far which could assist the defence.'

'Perhaps you'll allow me in due course to be the judge of that,' Mr Orkell said tartly, at the same time glancing at a note which his junior counsel had passed him. He nodded and once more fixed Nick with a severe look. 'Does the name Eric Bliss mean anything to you?'

'Eric Bliss?' Nick said with an air of surprise. 'No, I don't think I've ever heard the name, sir.'

'You don't sound too sure.'

'In what connection might I have come across it?'

Nick glanced at Donig who was watching him intently from the dock, leaning forward, his head slightly turned, as if he were deaf in one ear.

'In the course of your work as a C.I.D. officer,' Mr Orkell said.

Nick shook his head slowly. 'I'm sure I haven't heard the name before.'

'Would you be so good as to check on it for me?'

Mr Justice Finderson leaned forward with a frown. 'Surely the only check this officer could make is to ascertain whether anyone of that name appears in Criminal Records?'

'That's what I have in mind, my lord,' Mr Orkell replied.

'And supposing there is someone of the name with a criminal record, why should you be given the information?'

For a second or two defending counsel could only gape. 'It could be most relevant to the defence, my lord.'

'Hmm! All I'll say, Mr Orkell, is that I shall need considerable persuasion before I'll admit such evidence. You can't just pluck names out of the air, you know, and expect the police to serve you up with any information they possess on the person concerned. Whether Sergeant Attwell cares to check on this particular name is a matter for him, though I suspect that he will do so anyway. But I wish to make it clear that I'm not giving him any directions in the matter.'

While the judge had been speaking, Mr Orkell's expression had registered several changes of emotion, from which indignation emerged the winner.

'I very much regret,' he said in a stuffy tone, 'that your lordship takes the view that my conduct has been improper . . .'

'I never used that word,' the judge broke in.

'You implied it, my lord and . . .'

Mr Justice Finderson held up an admonitory hand. 'Mr Orkell, you and I have been around these courts long enough to recognise such small flurries for what they are, namely a ruffling of the surface waters and no more. I certainly had no intention of accusing you of any impropriety, my sole concern being to keep the trial within its evidential confines.'

'I am obliged to your lordship for those observations,' Mr Orkell said in a mollified tone.

Nick, who had temporarily stepped back into the wings while this exchange had gone on, reflected not for the first time that the legal profession excelled in humbug on occasions. However, the judge was certainly right in thinking he would be making a check on the name Eric Bliss. As soon as he could get out of court, he'd instruct Ted Cambridge to phone the Criminal Record Office.

Mr Orkell now informed the judge that he had no further questions to ask Nick at this juncture and Robin Mendip rose to re-examine.

'Did the accused at any time suggest that the revolver had been planted on him?'

'No, sir.'

'Did he have an opportunity of doing so?'

'Many opportunities, my lord,' Nick replied turning to face the judge, 'both at his room and later at the police station.'

'Thank you, Sergeant Attwell,' Mendip said, resuming his seat, 'that's all I have to ask you.'

A few minutes later as Nick was slipping out of court, he noticed Brenda Fulmer who was sitting near the door. She smiled at him as he was about to pass and indicated that she wished to speak to him.

'I thought you were wonderful the way you stood up to that old windbag,' she said.

'We get a fair amount of practice,' Nick replied. 'I wasn't expecting to see you here to-day, Mrs Fulmer.'

'I thought I'd like to hear a bit more of the trial. There's nothing wrong in that, is there?'

'Nothing. It's entirely up to you. You can come back every day until it finishes if you want.'

'I may do so.'

Nick suddenly observed that she had a small note pad and a ballpoint pen resting on her lap, partially hidden by her handbag.

'You'd better not let anyone see that,' he said. 'You're not allowed to take notes in court – or sketch,' he added.

'Why on earth not?' she asked, pushing the pad and pen further out of sight.

'It's against the rules.'

'How absurd!'

Having neither the time nor the inclination to argue the point, Nick excused himself and made for the exit. He wondered why she was making notes anyway, even though all he had glimpsed was a virgin page. What could it be that she was waiting to jot down?

There was no sign of Ted Cambridge outside the court, but one of the waiting witnesses said he had been there a moment before.

Nick nodded his thanks and made for a telephone. Luckily he got through to someone he knew in the Criminal Record Office who said that if Nick would call him back in ten minutes, he'd have the answer.

He wondered if it was too soon to phone Clare. It was only a few minutes after twelve and it was doubtful if she would be back. Nevertheless, he dialled his home number, only to hear it ring in an obviously empty house. He realised that she would probably pick up Simon and Alexander on her way back, which would mean she'd not be home until after one o'clock.

Seeing his side-kick through a doorway, Nick hailed him.

'I've been looking for you, Ted,' he said.

'So has practically everyone else, it seems,' Ted Cambridge replied.

'Why, what's up?'

'What's up! Only one witness failed to appear, another saying he's feeling ill and wants to go home, Mr Drinn phoning from his sick bed asking how it's going, Mr Bramber phoning from the Yard and saying he'll not be able to come along today as he'd intended and, finally, I've just had a call from Mr Walsh – you know, ex-Detective Inspector Walsh – to say he'd remembered something further about Harry Everett.'

'What's that?' Nick asked keenly.

'He heard at some divisional reunion a couple of months back that Everett's wife had walked out on him.' Observing Nick's expression, D.C. Cambridge went on, 'I know we know! But that's the sort of morning I've had. Anyway, what did you want me for, Nick?'

'It's O.K., I've done it myself. It was another name to check with C.R.O.'

'Who this time?'

'Eric Bliss.'

'Never heard of him.'

'Nor have I.'

'Is this another defence red herring?'

Nick shrugged. 'I'll know a bit more in a few minutes.'

'Jury all O.K. this morning?' Ted Cambridge enquired as

he turned to go. 'No overnight attempts to nobble any of them?'

'None reported.'

'Let's hope your Gordy picked a loser there.'

'It's still early days.'

As soon as D.C. Cambridge had passed on his way, Nick put through his follow-up call to the Criminal Record Office.

'Nothing in that name, sergeant,' the voice informed him. 'You haven't any other details?'

'None I'm afraid. Only Eric Bliss.'

'Then the answer's nothing. Sorry.'

'Don't be sorry. It's a relief in one sense.'

The voice laughed. 'Let me know if I can help further.'

'I will. Meanwhile, thanks.'

Nick returned to court for the final half hour of the morning. At one o'clock precisely, the judge would adjourn and be escorted away to have lunch with city dignitaries and other judges. Not for him the queue for meat and two veg, tray in hand, or the hastily grabbed sandwich.

Mr Orkell was cross-examining the pathologist as Nick slid back into his seat. The two men were not dissimilar in shape and size and faced each other across the court like Tweedle-Dum and Tweedle-Dee.

Mr Justice Finderson, for his part, had a slightly restive air, though whether from the onset of hunger or from a growing impatience with Mr Orkell, Nick was unable to tell.

When a short time later, the court did adjourn, Robin Mendip prodded Nick in the back as he was assembling his papers and said, 'What news?'

'C.R.O. have nothing on Eric Bliss, sir.'

'That's certain?'

'That's what they told me.'

'I suppose there's no reason why I can't tell the defence that, seeing it's entirely negative.'

'Any reason why you should, sir?'

Mendip smiled. 'No point in being bloody-minded just for the sake of it. Julius Orkell's all right.'

Nick refrained from further comment, but reflected on their differing attitudes. The answer was that birds of a feather did tend to flock together even if there were occasional outbreaks of fraternal pecking. But to Nick, the defence was the opposition to whom you yielded no quarter without a fight.

In fact, in the present instance he was perfectly happy to leave it to prosecuting counsel's discretion, particularly as he had considerable respect for Robin Mendip's ability to be scupulously fair without yielding any ground. Some prosecuting counsel these days were too wet for words and ran for cover at the first whiff of battle.

'Anything further to tell me about Everett and Blaney?' Mendip asked.

'Not yet, sir. Probably not until to-morrow. How long do you think the case will last, sir?'

'Depends on whether Donig gives evidence.'

'You still think he may not?'

'I now think it's less likely that he won't. Orkell's cross-examination of you seemed to be paving the way for his client to give evidence. And if he does go into the box, I'd have thought the case'll last another couple of days after to-day, possibly a bit longer. I gather, incidentally, that the judge can't sit on Friday, so it's fairly certain to go over into next week.'

Though Nick was intending to phone Clare during the adjournment, he felt that he would want to talk to her again in the evening when he got home before letting counsel know the result of her mission; assuming, that is, that it had been successful. They would also have to decide what to reveal about Clare's role in the affair.

It was for this reason that he had wished to hear Mendip's estimate of the duration of the trial.

As soon as he came out of court, he hurried away once more to the telephone. This time it was quickly answered and it was with a surge of relief that he heard Clare's voice.

'Hello, darling, what luck?' he asked, eagerly.

'Mrs Bishop *is* Mrs Blaney, Fulmer *did* visit her that evening, but she had absolutely no knowledge that he was going to be shot and had nothing to do with setting him up. That's it in a nutshell, Nick. I'll give you a blow by blow account this evening, but I can't talk for too long now. As it is, there's an ominous quiet coming from the kitchen. Hold on a moment, I'd better go and have a look.' In half a minute, she was back on the line. 'It's all right, they're drawing pictures. On some paper I've given them,' she added, not irrelevantly, in view of Simon's penchant for decorating floors and walls. 'But I mustn't stop or they'll start yelling for food. We'd only been back five minutes when you called.'

'What did you think of her?'

'I was impressed.'

'You think she's told the truth?'

'Yes, I do, Nick.'

'Why didn't she tell the police at the outset that Fulmer had visited her?'

'She was afraid of the effect it would have on their newly-constructed life. She knew she'd had nothing to do with his death, but realised it would be harder satisfying others of that fact. So she decided to keep quiet. I think I'd have done the same in the circumstances, Nick.'

'You've obviously done a great done job, darling,' Nick said, gratefully.

'You're not going to take any immediate action on what I've told you?' Clare's tone held a note of anxiety.

'No, we'll discuss that this evening. To-morrow will be time enough to do whatever's necessary.'

'That's a relief, because I promised her that everything would be done to avoid dragging her name into court. We must do our best to help her, Nick.'

'Sure we will,' Nick said, in a tone of greater confidence than he felt.

The trouble was that the decision what to do wouldn't rest with him. He would have to tell Robin Mendip, who would feel obliged to tell the defence. It would ultimately depend on whether Mr Orkell could be persuaded that Ella Blaney's evidence didn't assist the defence. It did not appear to do so, but would defending counsel accept that? On his present showing, the answer was a gloomy 'no'. On the other hand, Mrs Blaney had not committed herself to a signed statement and counsel were always extremely reluctant to call a witness who had not supplied a proof of their evidence. It was like playing the piano without a score and with someone having hummed the tune as one's only guide. Perhaps Mrs Blaney would refuse to make a statement in writing about what she had told Clare . . . All this was flashing through Nick's mind when Clare broke in.

'I must go, love. I can hear querulous sounds and also smell something burning. What time will you be back?'

'Not too late, I hope. Around eight with luck.'

Ted Cambridge was waiting for Nick when he emerged from the phone booth.

'I'm sick of this building,' he said. 'Let's go and have a beer opposite.'

The public house on the other side of the street from the Old Bailey always did a brisk lunchtime trade. The only snag was that you had to guard your tongue as you never knew who might not be waiting to pick up the crumbs of some incautious exchange.

'Let's go a bit further afield,' Nick said, 'and I'll tell you what I've just learnt.'

Ted Cambridge's reaction to Nick's news was to say, 'Good for Clare,' followed by, 'How are we going to sell this to the powers that be?' Nick noticed the use of 'we' and gave his side-kick a grateful look for his loyalty.

Tucked in a corner of the saloon bar, they drank their beer and munched roast beef sandwiches and discussed the permutations of Mrs Blaney's position until it was time to go back to court.

The afternoon was taken up with the evidence of a witness from the Metropolitan Police Laboratory who had examined the dead man's clothing and car and also a quantity of clothing which had been seized in Donig's room.

His evidence was long and tedious and the jury soon tired of gazing at each article as it was handed to him and he explained what his examination of it had revealed.

Their interest was slightly rekindled when Mr Orkell rose to cross-examine.

'You have told us that the deceased and the accused have entirely different blood groups?'

'Yes.'

'And on the deceased's clothing you found only blood belonging to his group?'

'Yes.'

'And on the accused's clothing you found a single blood

stain on a pair of trousers and that belonged to the accused's own blood group?'

'Yes.'

'And its position was consistent with a cut, or grazed, hand having rubbed against the side of the trousers?'

'Yes.'

'And you found nothing on any of the accused's clothing which connected him with your findings in respect of the deceased's clothing?'

'No.'

Mr Orkell sat down, sweeping the jury with a glance that seemed to invite a polite round of applause.

It seemed only appropriate that the judge should choose that moment to adjourn and lower the curtain on the scene.

As Nick and Ted Cambridge were leaving the building, Ted gave Nick's sleeve a sudden pluck.

'Look!'

A few yards ahead of them walking away was Trevor Lee and a few paces behind him a man wearing a cap. It required only a few seconds' observation to realise that he was shadowing Lee.

'He was standing waiting by the steps,' Ted Cambridge said, 'and fell in behind Lee as soon as he walked past him. I spotted him hanging round the court yesterday. Shall I follow them, Nick?'

Nick shook his head. 'Could easily be a wild goose chase. If he makes an approach to Lee and Lee reports it, that'll be that. If nothing's said to-morrow morning, we'll keep a further look out for the fellow in the cap. I take it you'd recognise him?'

'Oh, sure; with or without his cap. Whoever it is must have decided that Lee looks the most susceptible of the jurors.'

'We don't know that one or two others aren't also being followed with a view to an approach being made.'

Ted Cambridge shook his head in a puzzled way. 'Donig would need to have quite a mob behind him to organise it the big way and yet everything points to his being a loner. In which event who's got any interest in getting him let out?'

'If Donig hires out his services as a killer, he could be in demand. The fact that he freelances and is not a known member of any mob could make him very useful for a job as he wouldn't be associated with the rest of them.'

Ted Cambridge nodded slowly. 'I suppose it could be some mob leader returning a favour.'

'Quite possibly. It could even be the person who put out the contract for Stanley Fulmer.'

An hour later, Nick arrived at the café which was his rendezvous with Gordy. Their usual table was deserted and there was no sign of Gordy anywhere.

Nick ordered a cup of tea from the large-bosomed, impassive Polish wife of the proprietor and went and sat down.

It was Gordy's choice of meeting-place and Nick wondered whether the lady in question had anything to do with it. She was certainly built to Gordy's taste. If it were possible to arouse her emotions, he could imagine she would swallow Gordy whole.

Nick had just taken a sip of his tea when the door opened and Gordy came in, looking as though he had been blown through the door by a sudden gust of wind.

He gave Nick a quick smile and sidled up to the counter. When the woman placed the tea and ham sandwich he'd asked for in front of him, he glanced quickly toward the curtained-off opening which led to a tiny kitchen, and then leaning over the counter gave her right breast a gentle squeeze. The woman took not the slightest notice, but merely held out her hand for his money.

In a deep voice she said, 'Six p. the tea, twelf p. the sand-vitch.'

'My friend'll be paying,' Gordy told her and came across to join Nick. 'Poor Olga,' he said as he sat down. ' 'Er 'usband knocks 'er about.'

'She looks to me as if she could give as good as she got,' Nick observed.

Gordy chuckled. 'She 'as to put up with a lot.'

'So I noticed.'

Gordy frowned in incomprehension and Nick let it pass.

'What've you got to tell me?' he asked.

Leaning forward and putting his face as close to Nick's as he could, he said in an expression of warm, but mercifully harmless, breath, 'George Blaney's wife 'as moved 'ome. She could be living in Medina Towers.'

'What makes you think that?'

'Just something I 'eard.'

Nick, who had no intention of disclosing his own knowledge of the matter to Gordy, said, 'Where did you hear it?'

'Come off it, sarge, it's more'n my life's worth to tell you things like that. You just check and see if I'm not right.' He thrust his face yet another inch closer. ''Ave I ever let you down? It's because I'm good, you values me. Come on, sarge, admit it.'

It seemed to Nick that their recent meetings had been spent in his pressing Gordy for information while Gordy tried to squeeze praise out of him, with money in view as an immediate follow-up.

'What about Harry Everett?' Nick went on, declining the invitation to admit anything.

'You're a 'ard man, sarge,' Gordy remarked reproachfully.

'Harry Everett. Been able to find out anything about him?'

A sly look crept over Gordy's never exactly frank countenance.

'I might be able to 'elp you there, sarge.'

'Go ahead.'

'It'll be worth something.'

'We'll see.'

''Arry Everett 'ated Fulmer's guts.'

'That came out in court yesterday. I told you so.'

'No, you didn't, sarge. Honest you didn't.'

Nick now recalled that, in fact, he had not disclosed this fact, but had merely asked Gordy what he knew of Everett. So here, at any rate, was confirmation of a sort of what Brenda Fulmer and Neil Penfold had told the court. Moreover, if Gordy had been able to find it out, it meant that Everett's quarrel with his erstwhile solicitor was more or less an open secret in criminal circles.

''Arry Everett could be your bloke, sarge,' Gordy went on. ''E could be the bloke wot put out the contract.'

'We'd need to find some link between Everett and Donig,' Nick said, half speaking to himself.

Gordy's face came menacingly close again. 'P'raps there is

a link, sarge,' he said in a tone of self-congratulation. 'That interests you, don't it?'

'Go on.'

'I'll expect you to see me treated fair if I tells you.' Noticing Nick's impatient expression, he added, 'But I trusts you, sarge. You're a man after my own 'eart. 'Ow's your kid by the way? 'Ave you told 'im I'm getting a present for 'im?'

'He wouldn't understand.'

'You tell 'im that your friend Gordy's going to give 'im a present. Now what was we talking about?'

Nick drew a deep breath. Gordy had had his little revenge, which always took the form of hooking Nick's interest and then digressing into a sentimental memoir, or in this instance, more subtly, a reminder of the treat he had in store for Simon.

'We were talking,' Nick said, 'about a possible link between Donig and Everett.'

Gordy nodded keenly. 'What'd you say, sarge, if I told you they'd been part of a mob what did a bank a few years ago.'

'What bank?'

'Croydon branch of the City and Suburban Bank.'

'When?'

'December three years ago. Just in time for a Christmas share-out.'

'Anyone ever arrested?'

Gordy grinned. 'Not even the caretaker's cat.'

'Who else was on it with Donig and Everett?'

'There were three others.'

'Who?'

'Don't know that, sarge,' he replied, with a blank expression. 'It's not safe to know too much.'

'How can I get proof that Everett and Donig worked together?'

Gordy shook his head sorrowfully. 'It'd be difficult,' he said. 'But it's true wot I told you and it's the information wot counts.'

This was true enough in many circumstances, but, if anything was to be done about Everett, hard evidence would be required. However, Gordy's information obviously justified, indeed necessitated, a further call on Harry Everett.

Nick became aware that Gordy was staring at him with a hopeful look.

'That's worth a bit, in't it, sarge?'

'Something.'

'Like another cup of tea?'

'No.'

'Think I'll get meself one.'

He went over to the counter and called out the woman's name. She came through the opening from the kitchen and took his order. This time Gordy went no further than to give her forearm a quick fondle as she passed him his cup of tea.

'We'll settle up at the end, Olga,' he said.

'Have you found out anything further about the jury being nobbled?' Nick asked on his return to the table.

'Not seen them blokes since,' Gordy said, blowing on his steaming tea. 'But it's obvious now, in't it, sarge? If anyone 'as a go at the jury, it'll be 'Arry Everett.'

Nick had, indeed, been thinking along the same lines. Everett knew Donig, Everett had fallen out with Fulmer after a bitter quarrel, Everett hired Donig to kill the solicitor, Everett was ready to try and nobble the jury to secure Donig's acquittal. It all seemed to fit together. But who had grassed on Donig? Why, Everett. But if he had grassed on him, why should he be concerned to get Donig acquitted? It didn't fit, after all. Everett's name came up too often to be the right answer every time. Or if it was the right answer, a piece of the puzzle was still missing.

'I can see I've given you a bit of food for thought, sarge,' Gordy said cheerfully. ' 'Ow's the case going by the way?'

'O.K.'

'Donig?'

'What about him?'

' 'E not sprung any surprises?'

'He hasn't gone into the box yet.' Nick cast Gordy a suspicious look. 'What sort of surprises are you talking about?'

'Nothing, sarge. Nothing at all. I just wondered 'ow it was going. I mean, 'e might be suddenly pleading insanity.'

'No chance of that.'

'That's fine then, sarge.' Gordy looked up at the large, old-fashioned clock which was hung on the wall behind the counter. 'I 'ave to go soon, sarge, so perhaps we can settle up, as they say.'

'In a minute,' Nick said. 'I've got something else to ask you about first. Ever heard of anyone called Eric Bliss?'

It seemed to Nick that Gordy's reply came almost too pat and too quickly.

'Eric Bliss? Never 'eard of that name before, sarge. Eric Bliss, that's a new one on me,' he added, seemingly for good measure. 'No, I never 'eard of 'im.'

'Supposing I say I don't believe you!'

Gordy gulped. 'Not believe me, sarge? Why should I lie to you? All I've ever tried to do is 'elp you. Why, if it 'adn't been for me, you'd still be looking for old Fulmer's murderer. Now, admit it, sarge, that's true in't it?'

'Why are you so worked up just because I ask you about someone named Eric Bliss?'

'I'm not worked up because you ask about the geezer, but because you don't believe me when I says I've never 'eard of 'im. That's what's upset me.'

'You're being over-sensitive.' Nick reached into his pocket and produced three £10 notes. 'Perhaps these'll help soothe you,' he said, with a small sardonic smile.

The money vanished into one of Gordy's pockets with the same finality as coins being swallowed up by a fruit machine.

Nick stopped by the counter to pay the woman as they left the café. She took his money and handed him his change without a word. He wondered what did make her react. It obviously required something more than Gordy's furtive prods and squeezes.

They parted company on the pavement after making a further arrangement to meet and with Gordy, rather in the manner of an unctuous business letter, assuring Nick of his future best endeavours.

Nick watched him scurry away. He managed somehow to radiate wiliness even when viewed from behind. There was no doubt, however, that he was an effective professional informer with a wide network of contacts in the criminal underworld. Though he had a record of convictions running into double figures, he had never been in the big league. Nick could only hope, though without great confidence, that Gordy really had turned over a new leaf. Not because it warmed him to rejoice in one sinner repented, but because, if Gordy was still committing the occasional crime, it couldn't be long before he was caught. And when that happened, there was no doubt at all that he would expect Nick to get him out of trouble. Informers were wont to delude themselves into believing that *their* particular officer could give them one-hundred-per-cent, round-the-clock protection against arrest.

Detective Chief Superintendent Bramber had told Nick only recently how an informer of his had been arrested in the act of burglary and had reacted like an indignant diplomat claiming immunity from prosecution for illegal parking.

'You can't charge me,' he had said. 'I'm Detective Chief Superintendent Bramber's informer. Send for him.'

Nick dreaded the day when Gordy Warren should rub *his* genie's lamp and find that nothing happened.

CHAPTER NINE

Gordy had not gone very far from the café where he and Nick had met when he dived into a pub.

The barmaid who was not unlike an animated version of Olga gave him a warm smile while she continued serving another customer.

'Well, well,' she said as she came up to where he was standing at the counter. 'How's Gordy? You're quite a stranger. What is it, a Guinness?'

'A Scotch,' Gordy said with a pleased smile. As she turned to the rows of bottles behind her, he added, 'And make it a double.'

'You celebrating, dear?' she asked over her shoulder.

'Celebrating seeing you again, Hilda. 'Ave something yourself.'

'Thanks, dear, I'll have a Celebration Cream,' she said with a loud laugh.

She handed Gordy his drink and he added a couple of splashes of soda from the siphon on the bar counter.

'Cheers,' he said, raising his glass as she did the same.

'Life's obviously treating you well these days,' Hilda said. 'I'm glad it's doing someone good.'

'You don't sound too 'appy.'

'Oh, it's just I get fed up at times. I feel I'd like to go off to somewhere exotic with a big handsome man. But some hope!'

' 'Ow's your own old man?'

'When he's not asleep, he's in the betting shop or the boozer,' she said with a sigh. She eyed Gordy in a speculative fashion. 'I can't remember, you ever been married, Gordy?'

'She went off and left me after six weeks.'

'How long ago was that?'

'Eighteen years. She took up with an American airman.'

'You can only have been just out of your pram when you got married?'

'We was both seventeen.'

'And you've been divorced all these years?'

'Not that I know of.'

'You mean, she just walked out of your life and you've never even divorced her?'

' 'Ow could I? I don't know where she went.'

'You could have traced her.'

'I suppose so. Perhaps she's divorced me.'

'But you'd have heard.'

Gordy gave a shrug of indifference and drained his glass.

'Give us another,' he said, pushing it across the counter.

'Another double?'

'Yeah.'

'You are in the money, dear.'

Gordy chuckled. If he was not at this precise moment, he would be soon.

' 'Ave another yourself,' he said when Hilda put the replenished glass before him.

'No thanks, dear. This one'll last me. Well, tell me what you've been up to.'

'Just getting around,' Gordy said vaguely.

'I could do with a few tips if it means you can buy double Scotches.'

'No point in 'aving a bit of luck, if you can't enjoy it.'

'I certainly go along with that sentiment, dear. It's these people with stuffed wallets and long faces I can't take.'

'I'm not one of them.'

'I know you're not, dear. That's why I like you.' She flicked an eye to where a customer was waiting to be served. 'Don't go away, I'll be back,' she said to Gordy, as she moved along the bar. But when she looked round, only his now empty glass bore witness to his presence.

Gordy would have liked to remain longer, but decided that her probing of his good fortune was becoming an embarrassment. He liked Hilda, but had no wish to stay and be quizzed.

After leaving the pub, he wandered down Charing Cross Road and then made a right turn into Soho. He paused outside a shop advertising 'sex books and magazines' and then went inside. The man in charge gave him the same sharp-eyed scrutiny that all customers received. It was one of the shops where all the items were sealed in polythene so that only the outside covers could be seen, or in some cases where the magazine had been folded open, a titillating inside page.

Though Gordy had once worked in such a shop and knew the tricks of the trade from both sides, he walked out in disgust.

' 'Ow do you expect people to buy, when they don't know what they're getting?' he asked as he passed the hawk-eyed assistant on his way out.

'Piss off,' the man said, in a bored tone. 'Your likes don't buy anyway, you just come for a free look.'

A few doors away he stopped outside one of the striptease clubs of the district and glanced at the stills showing a number of girls in varying states of undress. A young man with greasy hair and several days' growth of beard was sitting on a hard chair just inside the doorway. His legs were stretched out and he was cleaning his nails in a desultory manner with an unbent paper-clip.

'Lovely girls. Brand new show,' he said mechanically, as Gordy studied the stills. 'Want something a bit special?' he asked in a lowered tone, as Gordy continued to linger, wondering whether to go in. It would pass an hour and he had time to kill. Eventually he decided to give it a try.

The young man took his money and pulled aside a black curtain behind him. 'Anywhere you like,' he said indifferently, twitching the curtain back into position.

The scene was not unfamiliar to Gordy. A small room with a tiny stage at one end and about ten rows of seats. Music came blaring from a speaker while on the stage a girl with a sagging figure went through various gyrations, from time to time casting away one of the veils she fluttered in her hands. Gordy watched with interest.

The girl finished her act to claps from Gordy and the only other two members of the audience.

A man came through a door beside the stage and went and whispered to the two men sitting in front of Gordy. Each in turn shook his head and the man approached Gordy.

'You like to meet Salome in her dressing room?' he asked in a foreign accent.

'No thanks, mate,' Gordy said genially.

The next three turns were different in form rather than substance, but they managed to hold Gordy's interest. He rather liked the look of the last girl, who was announced as Gloria and thought he might negotiate a backstage visit to her.

But to his slight chagrin, the invitation never came.

When he emerged, the greasy-looking young man was still cleaning his nails and didn't give him so much as a glance.

Gordy reckoned he might as well start making his way to the rendezvous. It was a tiresome journey by public transport, involving a change on the Underground and then a bus ride. But it was where they had met once before and the other person concerned had been insistent that they met there again this time. It certainly had all the virtues of a secret meeting place that suited both of them and outweighed the inconvenience. Anyway, inconvenience was a small price to pay in the circumstances. Indeed, Gordy would have been prepared to put up with far greater inconvenience if necessary. It was what lay at the end of the journey that mattered.

As he sat in the near empty bus on the final stage, he reflected on the ups and downs of his recent life. But at last he seemed to be on to something good. He might even be able to retire down in Kent, as he had always dreamed of doing, and run a pub. On the other hand, he wasn't really sure that, when it came to it, he wouldn't miss being part of London's murkier, but seething, scene.

The bus crossed a bridge over the river and Gordy got up ready to jump off at the next stop.

He walked back toward the bridge and then after a quick look in either direction, he scuttled down the steps which led to the towpath.

At the bottom he turned to his left and paused, peering beneath the span of the bridge. He coughed, but there was no answering sound. It was a quiet spot with meadows and playing fields on either side of the river and only the faint hum of traffic on the bridge overhead.

The greatest hazard was bumping into courting couples, but a damp, cold night would have driven most of them inside.

He walked forward a few steps on the muddy, uneven path and gave another cough as he came beneath the span. But still no reassuring sound came back. The lights on the bridge were reflected in the water, but beneath the bridge itself was like being in a dark cellar.

'Are you there?' Gordy hissed and gave a start when he thought he heard a slight movement ahead. 'Is that you?' he asked hoarsely.

'Yes, it is,' a familiar voice answered impatiently. 'You're late. How much longer have I got to stand here?'

With a sigh of relief Gordy walked toward the outline of a shadowy figure who had moved away from the protection of the wall.

'You got the money?'

'Here, it's in this bag. Take it.'

Gordy held out a hand and found his fingers brushing against a plastic carrier bag. He immediately grabbed it.

'You go first,' the voice said. 'Get on! I don't want to hang about here all night.'

Gordy needed no second invitation to leave and swung round to scuttle away. But before he could take one step, something was looped over his head from behind and bit viciously into the front of his neck.

He dropped the bag and clawed in vain at the constriction round his neck.

A single gurgle was his last and only sound and, as he sank to the ground, he heard a voice pant between laboured breaths, 'Nasty little blackmailer.'

*   *   *

Gordy's body was found about half-way through the next day, by which time it had been in the water for over twelve hours.

It was not more than half a mile downstream from where it had been thrown in, though it had first been carried some distance upstream by the incoming tide.

Then when the tide had turned, it had taken Gordy back past the point he had entered the river and deposited him on a mud flat where he was left amidst an assortment of old bottles and rusty tins.

He might have remained there much longer – or even have

been carried away by a further tide – but for a inquisitive and disobedient dog.

The actual position of the body was up against an overhang of the bank and out of sight to anyone who didn't clamber down on to the uninviting and smelly mud flat.

The dog in question had got down, but couldn't climb back up again. By the time its angry owner had slithered his way down to rescue it, it had found Gordy and was showing every determination not to be deflected from a long exploratory sniff at its interesting discovery.

CHAPTER TEN

Nick sat in court the next morning waiting for the judge's entrance. He was unaware of the additional complication the discovery of Gordy's body was to bring him before the day was out.

He was, however, suddenly aware of unusual activity in the jury box. Instead of their normal front of stolid patience, it seemed that almost everyone was whispering to his neighbour or stretching to converse with someone further away. They resembled a nest of birds threatened by a cat.

Eventually the foreman attracted the usher's attention and spoke to him under the watchful and puzzled eye of the clerk of the court. The usher nodded gravely and had just finished whispering to the clerk when Mr Justice Finderson made his entry.

Nick watched anxiously while the clerk held a murmured conversation with the judge, their bewigged heads close together like two blooms on a single stem.

Eventually the clerk turned round and sat down again and Mr Justice Finderson shifted his attention to the jury who had been observing the scene with mesmerised interest.

'Mr Foreman,' he said, 'I understand that you have something you would like to bring to the court's notice?'

The foreman of the jury, a middle-aged citizen of most respectable appearance, stood up and gave a nervous swallow.

'Yes, my lord. I wish to report that one of us was accosted on his way home last night.' He gulped and made a vague gesture in Trevor Lee's direction. 'It was Mr Lee. Perhaps it would be best if he told your lordship himself what happened.'

'Certainly,' the judge said, switching his gaze to Trevor Lee who now stood up.

'It was as I was leaving the station at Romford where I live. This man – I'd noticed him on the train – fell into step beside me and said he knew I was a juror and there'd be a grave miscarriage of justice if Mr Donig was found guilty. He made to go on, but I said I didn't want to hear any more and that he had no right to speak to me. He did try to say something further, but I walked away from him. When I glanced back, he'd disappeared. That's about it.'

Trevor Lee had spoken confidently and with an air which was clearly intended to convey that he didn't kowtow to judges or any other member of established society.

'You behaved most properly,' the judge remarked, 'both at the time and in bringing the matter to my attention this morning. Thank you.'

Lee sat down, with an expression of indifference to judicial flattery.

Nick reflected wryly how wrong they had all been in identifying him as the most susceptible to a successful approach. It proved yet again that you couldn't judge everyone by their appearance. Because Trevor Lee looked like a left-wing, anti-establishment figure (and very probably was) it didn't necessarily follow that he broke all the system's rules all the time.

Mr Justice Finderson focused his attention on counsel.

'The police will doubtless investigate this most serious attempt to interfere with the course of justice, but, subject to anything you, Mr Orkell, and you, Mr Mendip, wish to say, my own feeling is that least said, soonest mended. Mr Lee has behaved most properly and I hope that whoever it was that was so ill-advised to approach him will realise what a serious matter it is and that no further attempts will be made to influence any member of the jury to return a verdict other than one reached in accordance with the evidence given in this court.'

'I most heartily agree, my lord,' Mr Orkell said, squirming to his feet. 'The juror concerned is to be most warmly commended for the way in which he has handled this despicable approach. All I need say, my lord, is that my client had nothing whatsoever to do with the matter nor did he have any knowledge of it. The defence is wholehearted in its condemnation of what took place.'

Turning once more to the jury, the judge observed, 'You have heard what Mr Orkell has just said, members of the jury. There is, of course, no evidence at all that the approach to

Mr Lee was made at the instigation of the accused or anyone concerned with the defence and I would direct you not to hold it against the defence – or anyone else for that matter.' He looked at Mr Mendip. 'Do you wish to add anything?'

'Only this, my lord. I take it that your lordship would agree to a police officer – and I would suggest an officer other than one connected with this case – seeing Mr Lee with a view to obtaining a statement from him about this matter?'

Before the judge could reply, Trevor Lee had stood up again.

'Is it really necessary to make all this fuss? I reported it because I thought that would render any further attempts still-born. Personally, I have no wish to take the matter any further.' He cast a challenging look at the judge. 'And I take it that no one can make me.'

It is seldom that judges look surprised, other than by design, but Mr Justice Finderson was clearly taken aback. Worms may turn, but jurors never in his experience, save, on occasions, in their corporate return of an unwarranted verdict.

After staring for several seconds at Trevor Lee who had meanwhile resumed his seat, Mr Justice Finderson looked back at Mr Mendip.

'I think that the question of any police investigation had best await the conclusion of the trial. A decision as to what is to be done can be taken then.'

Nick reflected that this was probably as close to a judgment of Solomon as one of Her Majesty's judges could get. He regarded it, moreover, as a satisfactory solution from his personal point of view, in that it did not add to the existing problems on his plate. And the danger of any further efforts to nobble the jury seemed to have been effectively warded off.

After all this, the evidence of the first witness of the day came as something of an anti-climax. It was that of a uniformed officer who had found a spent bullet case in the gutter on the opposite side of the road from Stanley Fulmer's parked car.

Even so Mr Orkell found a few questions to ask him.

By the time the lunch adjournment was reached, the prosecution had almost completed their case. Mendip had already told Nick that, as the judge would not be sitting the next day,

Friday, Mr Justice Finderson had decided to adjourn until Monday as soon as the prosecution was closed. This would mean that the defence could have a straight run without interruption and that the jury would start with a fresh chapter on Monday morning. It would be fairer to everyone that way, the judge had told counsel out of court.

When the court did adjourn at lunchtime, Brenda Fulmer was one of the first to slip away. As she hurried off to the tiny restaurant she had discovered about a quarter of a mile away, she failed to notice that she was being followed.

Arriving at the restaurant, she was relieved to note that the small corner table she had sat at the previous day was vacant. She had seen how full the place became, hence her dash to get there ahead of the crowd.

Indeed, after giving her order – a cheese omelette as usual – she looked around and noticed that every table was already occupied.

She was in the act of reading the scrappy notes she'd made under cover of her handbag when she was aware of someone addressing her.

'Excuse me, but is this seat free?'

She looked up to find a pretty girl smiling hopefully at her.

Brenda returned the smile briefly and gave a nod. 'I'm afraid it's terribly cramped,' she added as she watched the girl squeeze into the second chair which was wedged between the table and a protruding segment of wall.

'I think I can manage,' Clare said as she cautiously sat down. 'They certainly don't give you much room in these places.'

'You wouldn't find me here, but for the fact I have to be at the Old Bailey this week,' Brenda Fulmer remarked, as if to make it quite clear to her table companion that she was not an habituée of such establishments.

'The Old Bailey?' Clare said in a bright tone. 'That must be very interesting. Though I suppose it depends what you're there for,' she added with a tentative smile.

'Supposing I told you I was a bigamist and that I've been let out on bail for lunch,' Brenda Fulmer said, relishing Clare's expression of astonishment. In fact, Clare had very little simulation to do, as the remark had taken her genuinely by surprise. 'It's all right, I'm not,' Mrs Fulmer added with a laugh. 'I'm sorry if I shocked you, but I'm always amused by people's reactions to rather outrageous remarks. As a matter of fact I'm there as an observer. I suppose the lawyers would call me an interested party.' She paused and fixed Clare with a curious little smile. 'My husband was murdered last January and I'm attending the trial.'

'Oh, how awful for you!' Clare said, disconcerted by the woman's gaze.

'I suppose you'd expect my face to be puffy with non-stop weeping, but it happened nearly six months ago and grief has to have a limit.'

'But you must find it harrowing having to sit in court and relive what happened.'

'I don't *have* to be there at all. In fact, I think the nice young police officer is rather shocked that I go on turning up when I could be sitting at home doing my crochet work or whatever he imagines widows get up to.'

Clare had considerable difficulty in maintaining her expression of innocent interest. Luckily, her plate of canneloni arrived and she was able to start eating. She wondered what Mrs Fulmer's reaction would be if she knew just what the nice young police officer really did think of her.

'I'm attending because I'm interested in finding out a bit more about my husband's death,' she went on. 'You don't find that odd, do you?'

Clare shook her head. 'Who murdered him?' she asked, feeling that this was the right question at this juncture.

'A crook called Clive Donig. But everyone believes he was a hired killer.'

Clare gave a small shiver. 'That makes it sound awful.'

Brenda Fulmer gave her a sceptical look. 'My husband was a solicitor and spent his working life amongst crooks. His firm specialised in criminal cases. You've probably read about the trial in the papers. His name was Stanley Fulmer.'

'Yes, I do remember reading an account, but I'm afraid I've not followed the case. So you must be Mrs Fulmer?'

'Brenda Fulmer. And you're?'

'Clare Reynolds,' Clare replied quickly. She always gave her maiden name on such occasions and it tripped off her tongue without difficulty. 'I'm a secretary with a firm of stockbrokers,' she added, before Mrs Fulmer could ask. It seemed a safe enough occupation to which to lay claim seeing that she was close by the district in which they operated.

Brenda Fulmer nodded. She obviously had no great interest in stockbrokers and even less in their secretaries. Indeed, it had become apparent to Clare that her chief interest was herself. The desire to talk about herself was uppermost and, as so often with such people, a sympathetic stranger provided an admirable sounding-board.

'My husband was murdered in rather strange circumstances,' she went on, 'and it's doubtful if the whole truth will ever be known. That's why I go along, to see if I can learn a bit more.'

'And have you?' Clare asked innocently.

'Names keep popping up,' she said with a mysterious smile. 'Names the defence have got hold of. One wonders what they've got up their sleeve.' She broke off and gave Clare a sharp look. 'Is there any reason why your face seems vaguely familiar?' she asked abruptly.

For a second Clare's heart stood still. It had always been a risk, albeit a minimal one, that Mrs Fulmer had seen her at court on the first morning. But Clare had not sat in her direct line of vision and had, moreover, been a face in a crowd.

When she and Nick had discussed the possibility of her getting into apparently fortuitous conversation with Mrs Fulmer, Clare had decided to alter her hair style in order to minimise the risk still further.

'I can't think so,' she replied in a tone as unconcerned as she could make it. 'It's probably because I'm a fairly ordinary-looking person. There's nothing very memorable about any of my features.'

'You don't exactly flatter yourself.'

'Well, I suppose it's better to look ordinary than have a face like a gargoyle that no one can forget.'

'There are other possibilities,' Mrs Fulmer remarked drily. 'I see you're wearing a wedding ring and I presume your husband finds you attractive?'

Clare gave a laugh. 'He seems to think I'm all right.'

Brenda Fulmer smiled abstractedly.

'A woman should never under-estimate herself,' she observed. 'I'm obviously mistaken and you're probably right in what you say about your appearance. Not that I mean that rudely. But I have to admit I've never been very good at recalling faces – other women's faces,' she added with a sardonically raised eyebrow.

Clare let out a silent sigh of relief. A crisis had been avoided and Clare chose the moment to engineer a minor quake at the table so that Brenda Fulmer's small notepad fell to the floor.

'Oh, how clumsy of me, I'm so sorry,' Clare said, bending sideways and reaching the notepad with outstretched finger-tips. She steered it toward her until she could pick it up.

'Thank you,' Brenda Fulmer said as she took it from her and popped it into her handbag, though not before Clare had seen the single name 'Eric Bliss' inscribed on a page.

It seemed that someone else shared Nick's interest in the person who went under that name.

Mrs Fulmer made no reference to the notebook and it had seemed to Clare that she had removed it from sight with undue alacrity. In the event Clare felt rather pleased with her small ploy.

'Has this man got any defence to killing your husband?' she asked in a tone of polite interest.

'None that anyone can foresee.'

'Perhaps he's mad.'

'He's certainly not that.'

'It must be horrible not knowing who put him up to it.'

'That's why I go along to court, in the hope of learning something.'

But there was something in Mrs Fulmer's tone which made Clare wonder if that really was the reason.

A few minutes later, Mrs Fulmer got up to leave. 'It's been nice talking to you,' she said as Clare moved to let her out.

'I've enjoyed it, too,' Clare said truthfully.

When the time came for Clare to pay her bill and depart, she found that Mrs Fulmer had dropped a glove.

'The lady at my table dropped this,' she said to the woman at the cash-desk. 'She may come looking for it.'

She felt that this tiny gesture somehow helped to fortify her bona fides as a stockbroker's secretary.

Outside on the pavement, she glanced at her watch. She need not yet make for home as Simon was taken care of until four o'clock and she decided to go and do some window-shopping.

The occasional free hour was now something of a luxury in her life and she was not going to waste it doing anything practical.

So long as she steered clear of the Old Bailey, she could wander at will.

CHAPTER ELEVEN

While Clare and Brenda Fulmer had been eating lunch at their shared table, Clive Donig had, as usual, had his midday meal in the cells below the court-room. He had scarcely noticed what he had eaten, his mind being entirely occupied with thoughts of his trial.

He had asked one of the prison officers to get a message to his solicitor saying that he wished to talk to him before the court resumed just after two o'clock and he awaited his arrival with increasing impatience.

Mr Naseby had spent his time sitting at a table in front of Mr Orkell taking notes which nobody was likely to need or to look at. Occasionally he had got up and standing on tiptoe had exchanged a whispered word with his client in the dock. He was a conscientious man who, despite a fairly extensive criminal practice, never felt really at ease with those whom he represented. The present case, in particular, had occasioned him many qualms and only his considerable sense of duty had enabled him to overcome his general feeling of distaste for much that he had been required to do.

'I understand you wish to speak to me, Donig,' he said, on being admitted to his client's cell.

Donig nodded. 'How do you think it's going?'

Mr Naseby frowned. Donig asked the question with the regularity of a hypochondriac taking his own temperature.

'Now that the prosecution's almost finished, I mean,' he added.

'I don't think I have any fresh comment to make,' his solicitor replied. 'Nothing's changed since we spoke yesterday.'

'I've been framed.'

'I know. That's your defence. That's the defence Mr Orkell has been laying the ground for in his cross-examination.'

'I didn't have anything to do with anyone talking to that juror.'

'The court accepts that.'

'If anyone did it for me, it was without my permission.'

'Quite,' Mr Naseby said, not wishing to hear more. 'Was there something particular you wanted to say to me?'

'This man Eric Bliss. It's important to find him.'

'I told you last night, the police know nothing about him. Prosecuting counsel passed that information on to Mr Orkell.'

'He's vital to my defence.'

'In what way?'

Donig bit his lip. 'He just is. He knows about the murder.'

Mr Naseby looked as uncomfortable as he felt. Defending criminals was like walking across shifting sands. Any moment they were liable to make some damaging disclosure which could place their legal adviser in an ethically untenable position.

'Do you mean that it was he who framed you?' the solicitor asked cautiously.

'Perhaps.'

'You've not said so before.'

' 'Cos I've been thinking.'

'You'd better write down a full description of him for me,' Mr Naseby said, with a renewed feeling of helplessness. 'Will you do that?'

'I'm not good at descriptions.'

'You must do your best,' Mr Naseby replied in a school-masterish tone. There was a limit to the number of wild chases on which he was prepared to embark at his client's behest, and searching for Eric Bliss fell within that category. He needed much more information before he would consider making a move to find him. If, indeed, he existed.

At first he had concluded that Donig was uncommunicative because he was too stupid to formulate thoughts. But later he had come round to the view that, though he was far from bright, there lurked a certain watchful cunning in his make-up. Deep behind his cold, impassive exterior, there *was* something which ticked away.

Of one basic fact, Mr Naseby entertained no doubt at all, even though many of its surrounding circumstances were cloaked in mystery. He was quite sure that his client was guilty as charged.

CHAPTER TWELVE

'I don't know how long I shall be out, Betty, but I'll definitely come back to the office. Don't hang about for me. Just leave a note on my desk if anything urgent arises.'

It was half past three in the afternoon when Neil Penfold thus addressed his secretary before setting off for his meeting with Frank Tishman.

When Tishman had telephoned during the course of the morning and said he wished to see him, Penfold had enquired when he would like to come to the office, only to discover that Tishman expected him to go there. His acquiescence had irked him ever since. Why should his late partner's brother-in-law have taken it for granted that he would hurry round there at the crook of a finger? He might expect his own employees to jump about meeting his wishes, but it wasn't even as if Penfold was his solicitor. Frank Tishman had never been a client of Fulmer and Co.

It was in a still grudging mood that he emerged from a taxi outside a modern building not far from Victoria Station.

He pushed through the glass doors and paused to study a board on the wall to his left. It was headed, 'Frank Tishman Associates Ltd'. Immediately beneath that in smaller letters was written, 'registered head office'. That, in turn, was followed by the legend 'Associated Companies' with a list of six. The only remarkable feature about the list was that each of the companies bore the name of Tishman, which confirmed Penfold's feelings about the man. He was an egomaniac.

He summoned the lift and rose to the fifth floor, where a receptionist told him that Mr Tishman would be free shortly. His guess was that everyone was required to wait, even though the boss of Frank Tishman Associates Ltd was doing nothing more profitable than making paper darts.

However, Penfold didn't have long to wait before he was ushered into Tishman's presence.

'Hello, Neil,' Tishman said, coming round his desk to shake hands. 'Have a seat and let me get you a drink. Whisky? Gin? Brandy?'

'Whisky, please.'

'I agree. It's the only drink for every hour of the day.'

While Tishman was fetching the drinks from a cabinet which seemed to be all glass and artful lighting, Penfold took the opportunity of glancing about his surroundings. With its expensive furniture and curtains and its thick sage green carpet, it was very different from any office at Fulmer and Co.

Tishman handed him a heavy, cut-glass tumbler in which the whisky seemed to nestle at the bottom like a precious elixir.

'It's a liqueur whisky,' he said. 'Over a hundred years old. I don't imagine you wish to kill it with water or soda.'

He went across to an armchair and sat down.

'Cheers,' he said, formally, holding up his glass. 'I'll tell you what I wanted to see you about. My wife.'

'Your wife?' Penfold echoed, when Tishman didn't go on.

'Yes. Has she been in touch with you?'

'I saw her at the Old Bailey on the first day of the trial.'

'Has she been in touch with you since then?'

'No, she hasn't, but I'm not sure that I can go on answering your questions without knowing the reason for your asking them.'

'We had a row the other evening and I thought she might have got in touch with you.'

'She hasn't. Anyway, why should she?'

'Because the row was about your late partner's wife, namely my sister-in-law.'

'I still don't see why,' Penfold said in a wary tone.

'Because she might have been checking up on what you knew about Stanley's domestic life.'

'I didn't know anything about it.'

'You must have had an inkling.'

'Of what?'

'Of how Stanley and Brenda got on.'

'As far as I know they'd reached a modus vivendi and there were no problems.'

'What does modus whatever you said mean?'

'They'd adapted to life together.'

'You went to their flat for dinner or drinks, didn't you?'

'Yes.'

'You're not telling me that you regarded them as a happily married couple?'

'No, I'm not.'

'You knew, of course, that Brenda was unfaithful to Stanley?'

'I knew nothing of the sort,' Penfold said hotly.

'I don't believe you.'

'I beg your pardon!'

'No need to get all indignant. Stanley must have given you some indication that he suspected Brenda of having an affair?'

'Well, he didn't. We very rarely discussed personal matters. Anyway, who is she supposed to have had an affair with?'

'Ah, that'd be telling, wouldn't it!' He stood up. 'Let me give you a drop more whisky.' He walked over to the cabinet. 'No question of the jury not finding Donig guilty, is there?'

'I hope not.'

'Though it'll still leave the sixty-four thousand dollar question unanswered. Namely, who paid Donig to do it?' Penfold said nothing and Tishman went on, 'Do the police still believe it was one of his clients?'

'As far as I know.'

'And you believe that, too?'

'I can't think who else it could have been.'

'Nor can I. It can only have been a client with whom he'd fallen out rather badly. I used to tell him that you couldn't represent the sort of villains he did without incurring risks.' He handed Penfold his replenished glass. 'What on earth made you ever join such an outfit?'

'That really is a remarkably offensive question. But, if you must know, it was because he was offering a good salary with the prospect of a partnership and I'd be running my own side of the practice – the civil side – without interference.'

Tishman gave a brief nod as if he had lost interest in hearing the answer to his question. For several seconds he stood in the middle of the floor, gazing out of the window. When he spoke, it was in a faraway tone.

'Personally, I doubt whether all the truth surrounding Stanley's death will ever come out.' He swung suddenly round and fixed Penfold with an intent look. 'And, in my view, it's as well that it shouldn't. It can't bring him back and truth for truth's sake has never been one of my mottoes. As far as I'm concerned my late brother-in-law has made an unlamented departure.' He gave Penfold a wolfish grin. 'And I suspect you're not too troubled either.' Raising his glass, he added, 'To our anonymous benefactor.'

Then observing Neil Penfold's expression, he burst out laughing.

CHAPTER THIRTEEN

That same afternoon, Harry Everett sat fuming while he awaited the arrival of someone named Tub. He had once been known as Tubby on account of his girth, but when he managed to lose some weight, one of his more waggish associates had re-named him Tub on the grounds that, as there was now less of him, something should be lopped off his no longer so descriptive name.

Everett was fuming not because Tub was late, but because he had just read an account of what had happened at the Old Bailey that morning in an early edition of the evening paper.

His meeting-place with Tub was a transport café near Shepherd's Bush Green, which was convenient to both of them. The fact that Tub was late did nothing, however, to improve Everett's mood.

Another twenty minutes went by before a worried-looking Tub appeared. He came straight over to where Everett was sitting and slumped on to a chair.

'There's been a bit of a hitch,' he said in a dispirited tone.

'You're telling me, there's been a hitch,' Everett said, tapping the folded evening paper which lay on the table in front of him. 'You've mucked it. You picked the wrong guy.'

'It's no good your being wise after the event, Harry. I did my best.'

'And a rotten best it turns out to be. Out of twelve possibles, you have to go and pick the one who immediately stands up and tells the judge.'

'He looked the right sort. How was I to know? You agreed when I told you about him.'

'I only had your description. You said he looked anti-police.'

'He did. He was definitely the one to go for. I bet you'd have picked him, Harry, if you'd seen him.'

'Well, I didn't see him and it was you who picked him and

now look what's happened. You might as well have built a thirty foot wall round the jury for all you've done.'

'That's not fair, Harry.'

'I trusted you,' Everett went on inexorably, 'because I couldn't be seen near the court myself and now the police are going to be buzzing around as if you'd coated their trail with strawberry jam.'

'No, they're not. The judge says nothing's to be done until the case is over.'

'Christ! You don't mean to say that you stuck your neck out even further by returning to court this morning? I must say I've heard of some idiots . . .'

'Harry, Harry,' Tub broke in reproachfully, 'I'm not that kind of fool. Now, just calm yourself and listen. When this juror gave me the brush off yesterday evening, I obviously needed to know whether he was going to report what had happened. So I arranged for my beloved to go along to court this morning and hear what happened and she told me that this juror told the judge he didn't want to make any statement to the police and the judge looked a bit narked, not being used to anyone talking to him like that, but said all right, nothing should be done until the trial was over and he'd decide then.' He threw Everett a triumphant look. 'It doesn't have all that in your paper, does it? So you see this juror wasn't such a bad pick out.'

'What are you on about? He told the court, didn't he? What's not bad about that?'

'But he won't help the police.'

'He won't help us, that's the point.'

'If he won't, none of them would have.'

Everett made a scoffing sound. 'You trying to tell me that not one of those twelve could have been got at? Of course, one or two of them could have. It's just that you picked the wrong one.'

'One can't back winners all the time, Harry.'

'When did you ever back one?' Everett remarked sourly.

Tub sighed. There was not much you could do about Harry Everett when he was in one of his unreasoning moods. No wonder he had always tended to be a loner. Nobody could stick him for long.

'Did Donig know that you . . .'

'Donig knew nothing,' Everett broke in curtly.

'You've never really told me why you wanted to fix his jury.'

'Because it's none of your business.'

'I can't help wondering . . .'

'Then don't!'

'Any idea, Harry,' Tub went on undeterred, 'who put out the contract for Fulmer?'

Everett frowned. 'Don't ask so many questions, Tub, they're not good for you. Anyway, what's it matter who put out the contract?'

'A lot of people are wondering about it.'

'Let them wonder! It wasn't me.'

But Harry Everett's denial did little to assuage Tub's curiosity. It would have done even less if he had known about Everett's bitter quarrel with his ex-solicitor.

Tub had always had his doubts about the success of the nobbling venture, but when Everett had offered him £100 to make an approach to the most likely candidate, he was not going to turn down the commission, especially as it was payment in advance, with the promise of more if everything went well.

Tub still felt that Trevor Lee looked the part and that it was pure bad luck it proved otherwise. Indeed, he was inclined to blame Lee for having let him down. It was unfair of anyone to look like that and not live up to it.

As things turned out, however, he had got his £100 for relatively little effort and minimal risk. The only risk had been at the moment Trevor Lee rejected his approach. If, at the same time, he had seized him and shouted for the police, it could have been a tricky situation, though one for which Tub was prepared. In that event he would have kicked his captor smartly on the shins and made a dash for freedom. The element of surprise would have been entirely on his side. And despite his appearance, Tub could be very quick off the mark when circumstances dictated.

Everett, who had been sucking a matchstick and looking pensive, pushed his chair back.

'I'm off,' he said. Then fixing Tub with an unblinking look, he added, 'Let's hope you're right and that nothing does happen.' His tone carried a faint note of menace, but Tub merely shrugged. It needed more than Harry Everett to intimidate him.

*   *   *

About four miles east of where Everett and Tub met in a café, Nick was in conference with prosecuting counsel in a room at the Old Bailey.

There were five people present, Robin Mendip, his junior Tom Parrod, Nick and Ted Cambridge and a clerk from the D.P.P.'s Old Bailey staff.

Nick had just finished telling them the result of Clare's visit to Ella Blaney.

Mendip frowned slightly. 'I'm sorry, but I'm not quite clear who went to see her. At one moment I thought you said a policewoman and later I thought you murmured something about your wife.'

'It was my wife, who also happens to be an ex police officer,' Nick said in an embarrassed tone. He went on hurriedly, 'As a result of the visit that D.C. Cambridge and I paid the woman, I became convinced that it needed someone not in authority, and yet someone who was used to that sort of interview, to get her to talk. I felt that if anyone could do it, it was my wife.'

'You were obviously right,' Mendip said with a quick smile. 'The question now is what are we going to do with this information? Let's take it in stages,' he went on after a pause. 'If we had known about it in advance, there's no doubt we'd have called Mrs Blaney as a witness to testify that Fulmer visited her that evening. And that's all we'd have needed to elicit from her. The defence would obviously have cross-examined her on the lines that her husband had a grudge against Fulmer, but, unless Julius Orkell is going to produce evidence that she lured him to his death and there's no indication that he has any such evidence, he can't take the matter much further.

'Obviously, if we don't apply to call her, the defence must be told. Indeed, we can't call her without serving a notice of additional evidence.'

'But she's not made a written statement, sir,' Nick broke in, 'so how could we serve a notice of additional evidence?'

'Just what I was coming to,' Mendip remarked in a faintly reproving tone. 'So the best thing would seem to be to let the defence know about her.'

'But supposing they decide to reveal her identity publicly, sir?' Nick said anxiously.

This time Mendip ignored the interruption, but turned to his junior counsel. 'I don't know whether you agree, Tom, but I think the best course would be for me to go and have a private word with Julius and ask him to accept Mrs Blaney's bona fides, unless doing so conflicts with his own information, and see what we can work out to protect her from damaging publicity.'

'I'd be most grateful if you would do that, sir,' Nick said.

'I'm sure that's the right way to handle it, Robin,' Parrod observed. 'And you can always both go and see the judge, if necessary.'

'I think it'll probably be desirable to do so, anyway. It's fortunate the court's not sitting to-morrow and then there's the weekend, so we have three whole days before we start up again.'

'Do you need to tell Mr Orkell that it was my wife who got this out of Mrs Blaney?' Nick asked in a worried voice.

'I think you must leave me to play that part by ear,' Mendip said in a not unkind tone. 'It's just possible that Julius won't be as interested as we assume. The defence have obviously been doing a certain amount of fishing during cross-examination, but when they see the dimensions of this particular fish we're going to hand them, they may back off. We can only wait and see.'

'Is Donig definitely going into the box, sir?'

'I think he'll have to, unless the defence are suddenly prepared to let our case go by default. I got the impression that they still haven't quite decided which option to take up. I think they're rather glad to have these coming three days to review their tactics. Julius Orkell is a fairly wily bird.' Mendip glanced across the table at Nick. 'Have you been able to discover anything about Eric Bliss?'

Nick shook his head. 'He's a complete mystery, sir. I've no idea who he is.'

At that moment, the door was opened and someone peered at the five men round the table.

'Is Detective Sergeant Attwell here?' he asked. Nick stood up. 'You're wanted on the phone.'

Nick excused himself and went into the office next door.

It was then he learnt of Gordy's death. Amongst the sodden contents of his wallet had been found a form from the local Health and Social Security Office. It was addressed to Gordy at the pub where he lived and referred to his recent claim for additional benefit in respect of his bed-ridden wife. It was not the moment to tell the officer at the other end of the line that the bed-ridden wife was a fraudulent figment of Gordy's imagination.

'But how did you come to connect him with me?' Nick asked.

'Your name was written on the envelope containing the form,' the officer said in a tone which clearly invited an explanation.

'He was an informant of mine,' Nick said.

He rang off after promising to attend the mortuary as soon as he could get away from the Old Bailey.

By the time he had returned to the next room, he had decided not to tell counsel what had happened until he had been able to put Gordy's death into some sort of perspective.

It was possible that it was not connected in any way with the Donig case. After all, Nick was not under any illusions about Gordy. He was a slippery, dishonest little man who would think nothing of running with the fox while he was hunting with the hounds. Nick had never been so naïve as to suppose that he had Gordy's undivided loyalty.

All that seemed certain was that he had met the end so often reached by those who chose to live on their wits in the twilight world of big crime.

Nick fervently hoped that it would be quickly proved to have had no connection with his current case.

Such was his hope. But his expectation was otherwise.

CHAPTER FOURTEEN

As they left the Old Bailey, Nick told Ted Cambridge what had happened.

'No need for you to come with me.' he said. 'Detective Chief Inspector Michaels of T Division is in charge of the enquiry and I'll tell him all he wants to know about Gordy.'

'I bet he could have done without Gordy's body coming to rest on his manor,' Ted Cambridge said. Then : 'When are we going to see Everett, Nick?'

'That can now wait until to-morrow. We don't have to go to court, so we have the whole day to tidy up the ends.'

'It still won't be long enough. Days never are. You're sure you don't want me to come to the mortuary?'

'Certain. There's nothing you could do. Have an early evening for once !'

'Thanks. I won't waste it,' he said with a grin.

'Don't turn up to-morrow looking as if you hadn't !'

Ted Cambridge laughed. 'I'm in good training.'

'For what?'

'Hockey and a few side interests.'

'It's the side interests that can take it out of you.'

'Don't worry, Nick, when you see me to-morrow, you won't know I didn't go to bed at ten o'clock with a glass of hot milk.' His grin broadened. 'Anyone hearing you talk would think you were old enough to be my father.'

'I'm all of eight years older than you, Ted. Eight experience-packed years, my lad.'

After they had parted, Nick found a telephone and put through another call to Clare. He had spoken to her as soon as he had got out of court and heard then about her lunch-time encounter with Mrs Fulmer.

'So it looks as if I'll be late again, darling,' he said after telling her of Gordy's death.

'That's an interesting development, isn't it, Nick?' she said, thoughtfully.

'One I could have done without. And so could poor old Gordy.'

'Yes, poor old Gordy!' Clare said in a tone that Nick knew well. A tone which indicated that her thoughts had chased off on a fresh scent.

'How's Simon been to-day?' he asked.

'He was a bit subdued when I collected him from Sally's. He'd got a bump on the forehead where Alexander hit him with a stick.'

'I hope he hit Alexander back.'

'You would! Luckily, Sally intervened and stopped the contest in the first round.'

'Is that the end of their beautiful friendship?'

'Good heavens, no! They really do have a genuine liking of each other. It's one of those chemical reactions you get in relationships, though not usually in children as young as they are. Sally said that Alexander was so overcome with remorse at what he'd done that he gave Simon a big kiss.'

'I'm not sure I don't prefer his hitting him,' Nick remarked.

Clare burst out laughing. 'I don't think Simon's genes will have been affected.'

Just talking to Clare on the telephone usually had the effect of raising Nick's spirits and he set course for the mortuary feeling more cheerful.

He was greeted on arrival by a young Temporary Detective Constable who told him that Detective Chief Inspector Michaels had asked to be informed as soon as Nick was there as he would then come along himself.

'Meanwhile, I'll take a look at the body,' Nick said.

'I'm afraid he's not a very pretty sight,' the T.D.C. said gravely. 'Dr Billing's expected in about half an hour. He's doing the P.M.'

Nick turned back the sheet which covered Gordy as he lay on a slab awaiting the pathologist's attention.

The face he gazed at was recognisable, but only just. It had a 'grand guignol' appearance fit for a horror show. His head looked as if it had come apart from his body and been poorly stuck on again, so that the slightest touch might dislodge it.

Nick was still staring at the gruesome sight when the door opened and a man of about forty came in. He had short, dark hair which was beginning to go grey and a youngish, pleasant face.

'Detective Sergeant Attwell? I'm D.C.I. Michaels. I don't think our paths have crossed before.' He held out his hand and gave Nick's a firm shake. Then nodding at the body on the slab, he said, 'Is it your informant?'

'Yes, sir. It's Gordy Warren all right.'

'Let's go into the office and you tell me what you know about him.'

It took Nick some time to relate all the events preceding Gordy's death. When he had finished, D.C.I. Michaels made a face and said :

'So it looks as if his death is tied up with the Donig case in some way. Once Dr Billing has finished the P.M., I want to go and have a look round the room where he lived. I'd like you to come with me. I didn't want to do it until I'd spoken to you, but I phoned the licensee and told him to lock it and make sure that no one was allowed in until the police came. He sounded quite a sensible chap.'

'He is, sir.'

'Meanwhile, we haven't been exactly idle,' D.C.I. Michaels went on. 'We're reasonably sure we know where he was killed. It was on the towpath beneath Chiswick Bridge on the Mortlake side. There are signs of a struggle having taken place and some partial shoe-prints in the mud, one of which, from a crude examination, could have come from the deceased's shoes. The lab'll be able to help us further over that. There's also a heel print from a different pair which could be important. I want to keep that fact secret as I don't wish the murderer to be alerted, otherwise he'll simply get rid of the shoes he was wearing.'

'If he hasn't already done so, sir,' Nick said.

'I agree that the prudent murderer will certainly have cleaned his shoes,' Michaels said with a wisp of a smile, 'but I'm hoping he won't have thought it necessary to destroy them. The towpath is frequently lapped at high tide and it's only because murderer and victim were right up against the arch of the bridge that their shoe-prints weren't obliterated by the water.' He paused and went on. 'Dr Male, who examined the body briefly where it was found, gave it as his opinion that it had been in the water around twelve hours. That would mean the murder took place say between ten o'clock last night and two o'clock this morning, give or take a couple of hours. It was high tide at one, so if the body entered the water before then, it would have been carried upstream before the tide turned and carried it down. For all I know at this moment, it could have gone backwards and forwards quite a time before finally coming to rest where it was discovered.'

'You seem to have found out a lot in a short space of time, sir,' Nick observed. 'Incidentally, Gordy didn't own a car and went everywhere by public transport. Does a bus route go near the bridge?'

'Over it. I've got someone enquiring into that aspect now. I'd have thought there was a reasonable chance that some-one'll remember seeing him. Buses aren't usually crowded at that hour.'

'Has your chap got a photo to show people?'

'There was a snapshot of him in his wallet. Showed him and a buxom female toasting each other. It appeared to have been taken inside a pub at Christmas. There were decorations and some holly in the background. I wondered if the woman might have been his ailing wife in respect of whom he was claiming benefit, but I gather not from what you said when we phoned you.'

'His wife left him soon after they were married,' Nick said. 'On the other hand, he was never short of buxom women. It was lucky you found the snapshot, sir, as you could hardly have shown people one as he is now.'

'You're right. It wasn't too badly damaged by water, either.'

They heard the main door open and footsteps in the passage outside the office.

'That must be Dr Billing,' D.C.I. Michaels said, getting up. 'Coming to watch him at work?'

Nick shook his head. 'I think I'll wait here, sir.'

Though he had witnessed a good many autopsies, Nick had never relished his attendance. Even less did he wish to see someone he had known dissected like a frog in a school laboratory.

It was forty minutes before D.C.I. Michaels rejoined him in the mortuary's small office, to be followed a few minutes later by Dr Billing who looked much more like T.V.'s friendly neighbourhood bank manager than someone who spent his days cutting up bodies in mortuaries.

Michaels introduced him to Nick and the pathologist nodded a greeting.

'I've told Mr Michaels that I have no doubt the deceased was already dead when he was put into the river. He was strangled by a piece of wire that bit deep into his neck. He was obviously attacked from behind because the main injury is to the front and sides of the neck. I would surmise that the loop of wire was thrown over his head and pulled tight almost in one movement.'

'Would it have needed much strength, sir?' Nick asked.

The pathologist shook his head. 'Not given the element of surprise. It was more a question of knack. Moreover, the deceased wasn't much of a physical specimen. I would assume him to have been below average strength.'

'He was quite wiry,' Nick remarked.

'That wouldn't have helped him if he was attacked in the manner I suggest.'

'Could one expect his assailant to have marks on his hands through twisting the wire?' D.C.I. Michaels asked.

'I imagine that he'd have worn gloves. Assuming, also, that he went prepared to murder, I'd expect him to have put a toggle at each end of the wire to give himself a better grip as well as to protect his hands. I suggest you search the area at low tide. The odds are he threw the wire away at the same time as he pitched the body into the river.'

'You say "he", sir,' Nick put in. 'Does that mean a woman couldn't have done it?'

Dr Billing was thoughtful for a moment. 'I confess I hadn't thought of it as a woman's crime. Though I have come across female stranglers in my time.' After a further pause he went on, 'As I've said, knack was more important than strength. Knack plus the element of surprise. In those circumstances, it could have been a woman who did it.' He looked from one to the other of the officers. 'Distasteful thought, isn't it, a cold-blooded female strangler?' Then turning to Michaels with a frown, he said, 'But didn't you tell me you'd found shoe marks at the scene?'

'That's right.'

'What size were they?'

'The heel print that wasn't the deceased's might have come from a man's or a woman's shoe. The lab may be able to be more specific. All one can say is that it wasn't made by a dainty shoe.'

'One wouldn't expect a woman to have worn dainty shoes on such an occasion,' Nick observed.

'Nor yet to have been a dainty woman,' Dr Billing observed drily. Then moving toward the door, he said, 'Well, gentlemen, I'll leave you with your problem.'

* * *

It had just turned eight o'clock when Nick and D.C.I. Michaels arrived at The Gaming Cock Public House in Camden Town, where Gordy had had part-time employment in the cellar and a room at the top of the building.

Nick had met Bert Hislop, the licensee, on a few occasions and quickly attracted his attention. He slipped away from the bar where he was serving and led the two officers through a door and up a flight of narrow stairs.

Handing Nick a key, he said, 'Don't mind if I go back down, do you? We're a bit short-handed this evening. That's his room up there.' And he pointed to a door at the top of a further flight of stairs. 'I'll be behind the bar if you want me, not that I can tell you very much. He went out about four yesterday afternoon and I've not seen him since. He never came back last night.'

'What time was it that you saw him yesterday?' Michaels asked as he and Nick began to climb the further flight.

'Half past six. We parted outside the café around seven o'clock.'

'So he never returned here afterwards.'

They reached the tiny landing and Nick unlocked the door of Gordy's room. As he pushed it open, the unmistakable smell of Gordy wafted toward him. It was the smell of unwashed-ness mixed with the dry, musty smell found in a seed merchant's.

It was a small cheerless room, which was also considerably untidy. The bed gave the appearance of not having been properly made for days, even weeks, its rumpled blankets hiding worse disarray beneath. There was a cracked wash basin in one corner with an ancient soap-caked shaving brush and a dirty razor propped behind the taps.

Opposite the basin was the only piece of furniture in the room, apart from a cane chair at the bed-head. It was a small chest of drawers resting on three feet and half a brick where the fourth should have been.

D.C.I. Michaels began opening its drawers. The top right-hand one contained various papers which Michaels glanced at and passed to Nick. They consisted, for the most part, of letters from various departments and branches of the Department of Health and Social Security replying to what had obviously been Gordy's claims for better treatment at the taxpayer's expense.

'Your Gordy seems to have been a fairly active fiddler,' Michaels remarked as he handed the last of the documents to Nick.

'He'd certainly try and squeeze money out of anyone.'

'And who better to screw than the welfare state !'

Not that it seemed from the correspondence that Gordy was always successful. Most of the letters asked for further information of his personal circumstances and some of the follow-up ones then referred him elsewhere. It occurred to Nick that Gordy and the bureaucracy were not unfairly matched.

D.C.I. Michaels pulled out the bottom drawer and rummaged, with nose wrinkled in distaste, through a mound of dirty socks and other clothing. His fingers touched something hard at the back of the drawer and he pushed the clothing aside to see what it was.

A moment later he had extracted a battered shoe box with an elastic band round it to keep the lid in position.

'Well, well !' he remarked as he opened the box and saw that it was full of £5 and £1 notes. 'So this was where he banked his money. How much would you say is there?'

Nick took the box and put it down on the bed.

'I'd say eight or nine hundred pounds, sir,' he said, after a quick riffle through the contents. 'There's three hundred in tenners at the bottom, and there must be more than that in fives.'

'Where do you imagine it came from? He can't have accumulated all that from social security fiddles or from the police informers' fund.'

'I don't know, sir. But I'd never doubted that he had quite a lot of irons in the fire at the same time.'

'We'd better have a word with Bert Hislop on the way out. Perhaps he'll be able to cast some light on the matter.' Michaels closed the drawer and bent down to peer beneath the bed. 'There's something under there up against the wall, but I can't see what it is.'

Nick got down on the floor and stretched out his arm. What came to view was a half-completed child's fort made out of match-boxes.

'I think I can tell you for whom this was intended,' he said, with a sudden catch in his voice. 'My son.'

He then told Michaels of Gordy's interest in Simon and of his oft-expressed intention to give him a present.

'If your son is anything like mine used to be at that age, it'll look more like an old heap of broken match-boxes than a fort by the end of one day. Come on, let's be on our way.'

Nick locked the door behind them and they descended the two flights of stairs. Putting his head round the door which led into the public bar, Nick signalled to Bert Hislop.

'Do you know anything about Warren's finances?' Michaels asked when the licensee joined them in the passage outside.

'He always made out he was skint,' Hislop said.

'We found that in one of the drawers,' Michaels said, pointing at the box which Nick was holding under his arm. 'It's stuffed with money. We've not done an exact count, but there must be nearly a thousand pounds.'

'The crafty old so and so,' Hislop remarked without rancour. 'The only trouble I ever had with him was when I caught him trying to borrow from customers a couple of times. I told him if he did it again, he'd be out on his ear.' He shook his head slowly. 'And to think I let him have that room for nothing because I believed he was skint.'

Michaels smiled briefly at the licensee's rueful expression. 'Do you know who his next of kin is?' he asked.

'He didn't have any family he kept in touch with. He lost contact with his wife nearly twenty years ago. She went off to America with some man and he didn't even know if she was still alive. And he told me that his only brother died in a brawl a few years ago. He always used to give my name as his next of kin.'

'Then I think it'd be as well if the money was counted now and we gave Mr Hislop a receipt,' Michaels said, turning to Nick. 'I'm just going off to the nearest police station to make a couple of phone calls, but I'll come back and pick you up in about fifteen minutes.'

With Bert Hislop watching him, Nick counted the bundles of notes. They had gone into Mrs Hislop's kitchen to do so and sat facing each other across the table.

'I make it nine hundred and twenty-six pounds,' Nick said, when he had finished.

Hislop gave him a bemused nod. 'Fancy his having had all that tucked away and my never knowing. He really was a crafty one was Eric.'

'Who?'

'Gordy Warren.'

'I thought you said Eric.'

Hislop nodded. 'He used to like me to call him Eric. And I did when I remembered.'

'But why?'

'He didn't think Gordy was much of a name. We were talking about names once and he said he'd like to have been called Eric and I said, "O.K., I'll call you Eric," and his face all lit up and he said, "Yes, you call me Eric." And, as I say, I did when I remembered, which wasn't all the time.'

'Did he ever give himself a name to go with Eric?' Nick asked eagerly.

'Not that I know of.'

'Did anyone else call him Eric?'

Hislop shrugged. 'Search me!'

'Have you ever heard the name Eric Bliss?'

'Never,' Hislop replied, giving Nick's rising excitement a cold douche.

CHAPTER FIFTEEN

It was just after ten o'clock when Nick arrived home that evening. As always, Clare came into the hall to greet him when she heard his key in the lock. They kissed and then she sniffed at his jacket.

'You've got a funny smell,' she said in a puzzled tone.

'It's from Gordy's room.'

'It's like fish meal,' she said.

'That's what Gordy smelt like.'

'You always said it was more like the mustiness of a seed merchant's.'

'I suppose it depends on whose nose. Anyway, you're getting Gordy's smell blended with Attwell, mark one.'

Clare giggled. 'Ready to eat?'

'Yes. I'll just nip upstairs and have a wash.'

When he came down again, Clare had their supper all ready on the kitchen table.

'Alexander gave Simon quite a crack, didn't he?' he said as he sat down.

'It looks worse than it is. He'd forgotten all about it until he caught sight of himself in the bathroom mirror when he was going to bed.'

'What did he do then?'

'Went through his Sarah Bernhardt repertoire of wailing and clutching his head.'

'It must have hurt him, poor little blighter,' Nick said, sympathetically.

'Well, if he wakes up in the night, you can go and comfort him and tell him what a brave boy he's been. He'll have no difficulty believing you.'

Nick gave a laugh and dug into his plate of stew. As they ate, he told Clare all that had happened since he had telephoned her.

'I wonder who Gordy went to meet after he left you yester-

135

day evening?' she said in a ruminative tone. 'It was obviously someone he knew. And why would they want to meet so secretly?'

'Presumably because neither of them wished to risk being recognised.'

'Or, more likely, that the murderer didn't want to run that risk. So if he specified the meeting-place, what inducement did he hold out to Gordy to go there?'

'That's easily answered. In one word. Money.'

'What could he have been giving Gordy money for?' Clare said, thinking aloud. 'It can't have been for future services because, in that event, he wouldn't have killed him. So it must have been for services already rendered. Or . . .' Clare paused in thought a moment. 'Or a blackmail pay-off.' She cast a glance at Nick. 'Is that possible? That Gordy was blackmailing someone, I mean?'

'Perfectly possible. He has no convictions for blackmail and I have no evidence he was blackmailing anyone, but it'd be quite in character. Gordy wasn't fussy where his money came from.'

'Then who was he blackmailing?'

'It mayn't have been anyone connected with the Donig case.'

'But supposing it was?'

'Who indeed? Penfold? Everett? Mrs Blaney? Mrs Fulmer? There's been absolutely no suggestion that any of them were being blackmailed.'

'Everett and Mrs Blaney are in a different category from Penfold and Mrs Fulmer. And, anyway, I'd rule out Mrs Blaney. I'm sure she's not a murderer.'

'I don't see Penfold or Mrs Fulmer in that class either.'

'Which leaves only Everett. I imagine he could have done it.'

'I doubt whether killing anyone would bother him unduly.'

'Of course, blackmail victims *can* act out of character. If they're sufficiently threatened, they *can* suddenly turn and lash out. It's happened. Incidentally, what about Fulmer's shady brother-in-law?'

'Frank Tishman?'

'Yes.'

'There's no evidence at all of his involvement. He's right out on the periphery of the case, if not further than that.'

Clare got up and removed Nick's plate, replacing it with a large slice of strawberry jam tart.

'It's curious that so many people seem to be interested in Eric Bliss,' she said in a reflective tone when she had sat down again.

'Who's interested apart from the defence?'

'Brenda Fulmer had the name written on her notepad.'

'Yes, I'd forgotten that.' He sighed. 'I really thought I was getting somewhere when Bert Hislop suddenly let drop that Gordy liked to be called Eric. I felt quite sure he was going on to say he was sometimes known as Eric Bliss.'

'Nevertheless it does seem a coincidence, Nick.'

'Not really. Eric's a fairly common name. Eric Bliss is one thing. Plain Eric is just nothing at all.'

For a time Clare remained staring thoughtfully at the sliver of jam tart she'd given herself.

'Even if you can only look at yours, I'd like some more,' Nick said, breaking in on her thoughts.

After supper, they sat watching television for a short time. Then Nick suddenly jumped up, switched off the set and pulled Clare to her feet.

'Let's go to bed,' he said. With a grin he added, 'We're wasting valuable time just sitting doing nothing.'

CHAPTER SIXTEEN

Ted Cambridge phoned the next morning to say he would call for Nick as it would be on their way to see Harry Everett.

He arrived about half past eight at the moment of maximum chaos. Nick had overslept and Simon was in roistering spirits which were not conducive to an orderly breakfast.

When the front-door bell rang, he charged ahead of Clare and waited impatiently for her to come and open the door.

'Hello, Clare,' Ted Cambridge said. 'Am I a bit early?'

'No, come in and have a cup of coffee and join the confusion. Nick'll be down in a minute, he's just shaving. But he's had his breakfast, so he'll be ready to go when he appears. He dropped off to sleep again after you'd called.'

Ted Cambridge now gave his attention to Simon who had been gazing at him with wide-eyed interest.

'How are you, Simon?' he said, holding out his hand.

'I wouldn't shake hands unless you want to be glued to him,' Clare said quickly. 'He's in the middle of his breakfast. Go and finish your bit of toast, Simon,' she added.

'I want to stay with the man,' Simon said, still gazing at Ted Cambridge.

'The man's coming to watch you finish your breakfast, but he'll go if you don't hurry.'

In the kitchen, Ted Cambridge lifted Simon on to his chair and then sat down beside him, while Clare poured him a cup of coffee.

'You've made a hit,' she said. 'He's usually rather shy at first with strangers.'

'I've got quite a few nephews and nieces around his age. I'm the youngest of five and the others are all married.'

'It can't be long before your defences crumble,' Clare said with a smile. She already knew from Nick how he bounced from one girl to another and it could only be a matter of time before he was caught. And a pretty good catch, too, for someone, Clare reflected as she watched him amusing Simon by pretending to snip off his nose.

'How did Nick get on yesterday evening?' he asked.

Clare told him about the visit to Gordy's room and he looked thoughtful.

'It's a bit far fetched to link Gordy with Eric Bliss simply because he liked the name Eric. On the other hand, who the hell is Eric Bliss?'

'That's a naughty word,' Simon said, waving his egg spoon.

Ted Cambridge looked mystified and Clare explained that the teacher at Simon's play school had banned various words, of which she imagined 'hell' must be among the milder.

'She must be very strait-laced to object to that,' Ted Cambridge remarked.

'She is, but she's also wonderful with the children. Nick and I have to be very careful what we say in front of him.'

It was at this moment that Simon dropped his spoon and said 'bugger' in a loud voice.

Clare looked at Ted Cambridge with an expression of comical dismay. 'I do promise you he hasn't picked that word up at home,' she said, while Simon got down on the floor and then began crawling beneath the table. 'There's an angelic-looking child called Lionel whose father swears like the proverbial trooper. I'm sure Miss Turpin, that's the teacher, has had her vocabulary considerably broadened since Lionel's arrival.'

'Nobody under middle-age ought to be called Lionel, anyway,' Ted Cambridge said. 'I think there's a lot to be said for being able to change your name when you grow up. Some names simply don't fit children and others don't fit adults.'

Simon emerged at the other end of the table and Clare led him across to the sink and wiped his face and hands.

'Go and tell Daddy to hurry up,' she said, and he shot away out of the door.

'Daddy, Daddy,' he shrieked as he went.

'Have you ever heard a child speak quietly?' Clare said, with a sigh.

'Stop shouting!' Nick bellowed from somewhere upstairs, as Simon approached.

A couple of minutes later, they arrived hand in hand in the kitchen.

' 'Morning, Ted. Sorry to have kept you. Did Clare explain? I'm ready, if you are.'

Ted Cambridge finished his coffee and got up while Nick kissed his wife and son good-bye.

'Get ready, Simon,' Clare said. 'It's time for us to go too.'

'I don't want to go to school,' Simon announced.

'Yes you do,' his parents said in unison.

'I want to stay with the man.'

'The man's going with Daddy,' Clare said. 'Moreover he has a name. Call him Ted.'

'Ted,' Simon said, as though trying the name out and liking its sound. 'Why are you called Ted?'

'Why are you called Simon?' Ted Cambridge countered.

'It's my name.'

'Ted's mine.'

'Ted.'

'That's right. Good-bye, Clare, thanks for the coffee. Good-bye, Simon.' And he hurried after Nick who was waiting by the front door.

'We might as well try his home first,' Nick said as they drove off. 'If he's not there, we'll go on to his place of work. You've got the address?'

'Yes. The local station gave it me. I gather they like to keep a general eye on him, though they have to be fairly careful not to give him any cause for complaining that he's being harassed by the law.'

They arrived outside Number 48 in the drab street in which Everett lived and got out of the car. After ringing and banging on the door without any response, they decided that he had already left for work.

A couple of minutes later, they were on their way to an address off Shepherd's Bush Road where he worked. The premises turned out to be a yard with a prefab shed at one end and a small office beside the entrance. A door bore the legend 'Enquiries' and they entered.

A middle-aged woman in a home-knitted sweater was in the act of making tea.

'I'll be with you in a moment,' she said over her shoulder,

as she continued pouring water from the steaming kettle into the teapot.

Ted Cambridge glanced at Nick and gave a helpless shrug.

'Yes, can I help you?' she asked, at last turning round and facing them.

'We're looking for Harry Everett. We understand that he works here.'

The woman looked flustered. 'Oh, dear, I think you'd better speak to the foreman. I'll see if I can find him. I know he's about as he was in here a few minutes ago. I expect he's somewhere in the yard.'

Leaving them standing at a small counter, she exited through a side door and disappeared round a corner of the building. It was not long before she reappeared, accompanied by a tough, red-faced man in overalls.

'This is the foreman,' she said before quickly turning back to her tea-making.

'What can I do for you?' the man asked in a suspicious voice.

'We're looking for Harry Everett.'

'Who are you?'

'Police.'

'I guessed as much. Well, he isn't here.'

'Doesn't he work here?'

'He did.'

'When did he leave?'

'He never put in an appearance yesterday and he hasn't come to-day.'

'And he hasn't been in touch with you?'

'He phoned yesterday morning and said he wouldn't be in for a few days.'

'Did he say why not?'

'He just said something sudden had cropped up.' The man looked belligerently from one to the other. 'I told him if he wasn't in this morning, he needn't bother to come back. As far as I'm concerned, he's finished here.'

'He gave you no clue as to exactly what had cropped up?' Nick said.

'None.'

'Did you ask him?'

'No. Wasn't any of my business. And anyway, he'd have told me if he wanted me to know.'

Nick gave a thoughtful nod. 'If he does turn up, will you call me at this number?'

He scribbled his Yard telephone number on a scrap of paper and handed it to the foreman.

'It's quite likely I won't be there, but someone'll take a message.'

The man glanced at the number and put the piece of paper on the cluttered desk beside him.

'If that's all, I've got work to do,' he said.

'Thanks for your help,' Nick said in a matching tone.

'I don't think he cares for the police,' Ted Cambridge remarked, as they drove away.

'I didn't get the impression that he cared for anyone,' Nick replied.

Fifteen minutes later, they were back outside Everett's house, which was managing to look more unoccupied than ever. The downstairs front-room curtains were drawn across the window and those at the upstairs window were partially drawn.

A passage ran down the detached side of the house.

'We'll go and explore the back,' Nick said.

'Wouldn't be difficult to break in,' Ted Cambridge remarked as they examined the rear of the premises.

They became aware of a woman watching them from a window in the neighbouring house and Nick walked to the dividing fence and called to her. A few seconds later, she opened her back door and came out on to the step. She was wearing a green nylon overall and her hair was done up in a head scarf.

'Excuse me, madam, but do you know where Mr Everett is?' She shook her head. 'In't he at work?'

'Apparently not. When did you last see him?'

'Don't see him often. He keeps himself to himself. Good job too after the way he spoke to my husband. It was on account of his throwing out rubbish and the wind blowing it into our garden. My husband spoke to him about it and he was ever so crude.' She paused, before adding in a withering tone, 'We may live next door, but we're not neighbours like me and Mrs Foster are on the other side. You the police or something?'

'Police.'

'Why don't you break in and see what's happened? He may be dead,' she said hopefully.

'How long has he lived here?'

'Not above a year. His wife left him not long after they moved in. Don't blame her either.'

'I reckon that, with a good bunch of keys, we can get in,' Ted Cambridge said quietly to Nick. 'I've got a bunch out in the car. Shall we have a try?'

Nick nodded. He reckoned that he would be able to justify the entry, should any complaint be made. But who was likely to complain apart from Everett himself? And the chance that he would do so was remote. He might even be dead, as the woman next door so patently hoped. Anyway, the police urgently needed to interview him.

Ted Cambridge returned with a bunch of long, slim keys and began trying them in the lock of the back door, which was fortunately out of view of the woman, who had gone back inside her house but was still peering from a window.

The third key turned in the lock and they entered to find themselves in a tiny scullery. The sink was full of unwashed crockery and there was a gas cooker which looked as if it had never been cleaned. Next to the scullery was the kitchen which had been converted into a back parlour. The door from this opened on to the short passage leading to the front door. On the left of the passage lay the front room, whose curtains were drawn.

Nick opened the door and switched on the light. There was no one inside and the room looked precisely as it had when they had called on Harry Everett a few evenings before.

'Let's take a look upstairs,' Nick said.

There were two rooms and a bathroom. One of the rooms was completely bare of furniture, but the front one was furnished as a bedroom with the bed itself made in a sort of way. At any rate, it didn't appear to have been recently slept in. Nick felt the pillow which was quite cold.

The scruffy pair of slippers he remembered Everett wearing when they had visited him lay on the floor; but apart, as if they had quarrelled.

Nick looked around for other shoes. There was a pair of

143

canvas, rope-soled ones over in a corner and close by a pair of outdoor black leather slippers with ornamental gold-buckles. None of them looked like the sort of footwear for meeting someone on a muddy towpath late at night. Nevertheless, he picked up each shoe in turn and examined its sole. The canvas pair could not have made the heel mark which D.C.I. Michaels had described and the black leather slippers appeared almost new. They bore no sign of scuffing or of having undergone recent cleaning. Indeed, Nick found that they were covered by an undisturbed film of dust.

So much for Harry Everett's footwear, apart from whatever he was wearing at this moment. It had been worth investigating, but they had drawn a blank.

'Nothing in the bathroom,' Ted Cambridge announced, returning to the bedroom where Nick was completing his search. 'Except for a dead spider in the bath which looks quite at home there.'

'We'll leave the same way as we entered,' Nick said, as they went back downstairs.

It was when they were back in the scullery and he was immediately behind Ted Cambridge, who was unlocking the door to let them out, that he suddenly noticed a pair of galoshes beneath the sink.

He bent down and picked them up. They gave the appearance of having been washed, but not thoroughly. There were faint traces of mud round the heels and some caked bits adhering to the instep of each.

'What size would you call them, Ted?'

'Medium,' Ted Cambridge said, after a thoughtful look.

'We'll take them with us. Have you got something in the car we can wrap them in?'

'Yes, any number of plastic shopping bags. I'll fetch a couple.'

When he returned with the bags, he found Nick frowning in a worried manner.

'What's up?'

'If these galoshes were worn by the murderer, you know what Everett's going to say?'

'That they were planted here by police?'

'Precisely.'

'It'll be our word against his. Anyway, we've first to find Everett. What do you want to do next, Nick?'

'Hand these to D.C.I. Michaels. After all, it's his investigation.'

'And then?'

'I was thinking we might pay a visit to Fulmer and Co.'

* * *

Neil Penfold looked drawn and nervous. Nick surmised that he was still suffering the after-effects of the mauling he had received in court. Moreover, an unannounced visit from the police had probably contributed to his general state of nervousness. He had certainly been left in a most unenviable position as a result of his senior partner's dramatic demise, not that Nick was inclined to accord him much sympathy when he recalled the barriers of non-co-operation Penfold had erected during the investigation of Stanley Fulmer's death.

Penfold now looked anxiously from Nick to Ted Cambridge as if certain that their presence could only mean more bad news.

'We thought we'd look in as we were in the neighbourhood,' Nick said disarmingly. 'There hasn't been an opportunity to talk to you since you gave evidence.'

'I heard the court wasn't sitting to-day,' Penfold said, making their conversation appear to jump a move. 'Mrs Fulmer told me.'

'She's been along every day. She seems peculiarly interested. Even takes notes when no one's watching.' Nick paused. 'I wonder why she's so keen to be there. Have you any idea?'

Penfold shook his head vigorously. 'I'm sure there's nothing mysterious about her attendance. She just wants to find out as much as she can about her husband's death.'

'Taking notes seems a bit strange, doesn't it?'

'So many names get mentioned in the course of evidence, I suppose she jots them down to avoid subsequent confusion. I'm sure there's nothing sinister in it.'

'You're obviously in touch with her?' Nick said.

'She phones me from time to time.' He paused and then added, as if feeling that further explanation was required,

'I'm handling her affairs. As you know, Mr Fulmer's will was entirely in her favour, but it's being a complicated business obtaining probate. The valuation of his share of the partnership is proving a nub of contention with the authorities, but no more than expected.'

'Anyway, Mrs Fulmer is well provided for, is she?'

'Amply.'

'However, I didn't really come here to talk about Mrs Fulmer. I came to find out if you had unearthed anything further about those two clients whose names were shown to you on a piece of paper?'

'Blaney and Everett?'

'Yes. I'm sure you must have looked through your files on them, haven't you?' Penfold appeared to hesitate and Nick went on, 'Well, haven't you? It'd be very odd if you hadn't.'

'Naturally, I've taken the opportunity of doing so.'

'And?'

'There's nothing in them that would help the court. You can have my word for that.'

'Are you willing to let us see them?'

'You know I can't let you do that, Mr Attwell, we've been through it all before. As a matter of principle I must claim solicitor–client privilege.'

'It could be waived.'

'I doubt whether I have authority to waive it on behalf of my deceased partner and I doubt even more whether the two clients concerned would be prepared to waive their privilege.'

'I think I'd agree with you about that,' Nick said, with a sigh.

'I don't see how George Blaney can have had anything to do with the murder. After all, he's in the security wing at Parkhurst, his letters are censored and his visitors are vetted. You'd know if he'd tried to organise anything from inside prison.'

'You know he felt that Mr Fulmer had deliberately shopped him?'

'Yes,' Penfold said in a cautious tone.

'Was Mr Fulmer upset by the accusation?'

'I couldn't tell you.'

'Couldn't you? Didn't Mrs Blaney report his conduct to the Law Society?'

'Yes, but the Law Society receives hundreds of unfounded complaints from disgruntled clients.'

'And some well-founded ones, too, I'm sure.'

'A few, perhaps. But it would have been grossly unethical of Mr Fulmer to have behaved in the way alleged by Blaney.'

'I respect your loyalty to your dead partner, Mr Penfold, but does it really have to extend to pretending that he never did anything unethical?'

'As I've explained to you countless times, Mr Attwell, Mr Fulmer and I worked largely in watertight compartments.'

'But you knew about Blaney's accusation?'

'Yes, because Mr Fulmer felt it proper to consult me when the complaint reached an official level. After all, not just he, but the firm's good name was involved.'

Nick refrained from asking when Fulmer and Co. had ever had a good name.

'Would it surprise you to know that Mr Fulmer visited Mrs Blaney on the night he was murdered?'

Penfold's expression was one of bewilderment giving way to consternation.

'Why . . . how did you . . . oh lord, what's all this going to mean now? Haven't I borne the brunt of enough?'

'We might have found out sooner, if you'd been more helpful.' Nick held up a hand. 'All right, I know! Solicitor–client privilege locked your files and sealed your lips. Anyway, I take it you are surprised?'

'I've told you and I've told the court, I had no idea where he was going that evening. So it was to see Mrs Blaney, was it? Does that mean she lives in Medina Towers?'

'Yes, under an assumed name. Are you certain there's no letter in the Blaney file showing that she wrote from a Medina Towers address?'

'Quite certain. I'd have noticed at once and told you.'

'Would you? Would you really have told us?'

Beads of perspiration showed on Penfold's forehead.

'Mr Attwell, I know you don't believe me half the time, but I can promise you that it's been like sitting on a keg of dynamite here ever since Stanley Fulmer's death. O.K., I'll admit he was up to all sorts of dirty tricks. Everyone knew it, so why shouldn't I admit it? I'm sick of being treated as if I was his collaborator in all the shadier things he undertook. I wasn't. He was at it long before I joined the firm.'

'But you did join the firm and you did become his partner,' Nick said flatly. 'And I assume that both were voluntary actions on your part.'

'I'm beginning to rue the day.'

'Isn't it a bit late to do that?'

'All right, I know it's useless trying to get you to understand my difficulties, but it's other people I've had to think about all the time. Clients.' He let out a shuddering sigh. 'To get back to Mrs Blaney. As I've said, I didn't know he was intending to visit her that evening. On the other hand, I'm not wholly surprised, because I do know he was most anxious to persuade her that she and George Blaney were quite wrong in believing he had sold George down the river.'

'Why was he especially bothered about this particular allegation of chicanery?'

'I don't know.'

'Might it have been because he thought it could be proved?'

Penfold shrugged helplessly. 'He used to maintain numerous contacts, none of which were ever recorded in writing, so I just don't know. He was constantly receiving mysterious phone calls and popping out of the office to meet people. That was the way he operated on behalf of his clients. Nothing would be put into writing which might later prove dangerous.' He looked at Nick as if seeing him in some new light. 'I don't have to tell you that! The police knew as well as anyone, and better than most, what he got up to. Or if they didn't know, they suspected.'

'Suspicion is one thing, evidence is another.'

'The police probably had as strong a motive as anyone to see him put out of circulation. He was fully aware of that. Hence the practice of not recording anything which could be damaging if it ever came to light.'

'To say that the police were happy to see him put out of circulation doesn't mean they had a motive to arrange his death. To see him put behind bars was as far as their hopes ran.'

'Oh, I'm not suggesting that you put out the alleged contract.' With a twisted little smile, he added, 'Though, from all I've seen, you're not exactly shy about the use of dirty tricks yourselves. But, of course, you only employ them in the public interest. Or so you'd say.' The smile became momentarily malevolent. 'I'm not trying to needle you; only point out that, in my experience, few people, if any, are wholly black or purest white. Most are a shade of grey.'

'By that token,' Ted Cambridge remarked, 'Mr Fulmer must have been the colour of my first pair of flannel shorts, charcoal grey.'

Penfold made a small throwaway gesture with his hand as if to indicate that the comment wasn't worthy of reply.

'This has all been very interesting,' Nick said, 'but now let's get back to basics. We haven't yet discussed the other name on the piece of paper. Harry Everett.'

'From all I can learn, Everett was even more bitter toward Mr Fulmer than Blaney.'

'Because Mr Fulmer cheated him out of a large sum of money?'

'That's right. Or rather that's the allegation.'

'It probably is right, too. And if it was part of the proceeds of a robbery, Everett would have no redress. He couldn't go to the police and he couldn't tell anyone without admitting he had committed a robbery of which a jury had acquitted him. He mightn't be tried again for the offence; indeed he couldn't be, but he could still have been charged with perjury. So that meant Harry Everett was left to his own devices.'

'If anyone hired Donig, I would think Everett the most likely candidate,' Penfold remarked.

'I'm interested to hear you say that,' Nick said thoughtfully.

'It's only surmise, mind you.' Penfold appeared to deliberate a moment. 'As a matter of fact, I heard a rumour a couple of days ago that Everett and Donig once worked with the same firm. Percy, our chief clerk, picked it up on a side wind when he was visiting a client at Brixton the other evening. I feel able to tell you because it has nothing whatsoever to do with the client's case. Nevertheless, I wouldn't want Percy to know that I had told you or even that I had talked to you in this manner. He remains intensely loyal to Mr Fulmer's memory.

Of course, he worked with him much more closely than I did and he had also known him much longer.'

Nick nodded, but said nothing. It seemed that a small crack had suddenly appeared in the façade of Fulmer and Co. He had no intention of disclosing that he had received similar information about a link between Everett and Donig.

'Before we leave, there is one other person I want to ask you about, Mr Penfold,' he said. 'Ever heard of Eric Bliss?'

The solicitor shook his head slowly. 'No, I haven't,' he said, with a frown.

'Can you be sure that no one of that name has ever been a client of your firm?'

'If you hang on a moment, I'll check in the accounts section.'

'That'd be very obliging of you,' Nick said, unable to keep a faint note of surprise from his voice. After Penfold had left the room, he looked at Ted Cambridge and said, 'What do you make of his performance this morning?'

'I think it's all summed up when he says he's sitting on a keg of dynamite. I believe he's scared stiff of being blown sky high if only a fraction of Fulmer's misdeeds comes to light. And I think he's just realised that he may need a few friends if that does happen.'

'Could be you're right, Ted,' Nick said, as Penfold came back into the room.

'We have no record of having ever had a client of that name,' he said.

'I suppose you don't keep a record of your clients' aliases, do you?'

Penfold smiled wanly. 'When known, they're cross-referenced,' he said. 'But I've checked that, too, and there's nothing.'

Shortly afterwards, the two officers departed. As they returned to their car, Ted Cambridge said, 'I'd give a lot to get my hands on their register of aliases. I reckon it'd provide even better reading than a Swiss bank's list of its foreign customers.'

'And be as strenuously protected from prying eyes as well,' Nick observed.

*　　*　　*

At about the same time as Nick and D.C. Cambridge were leaving the office of Fulmer and Co., Robin Mendip was strolling from his own chambers to those of Julius Orkell, which were in a different part of the Temple.

'Come in, Robin, and sit down,' Orkell said, as prosecuting counsel was ushered into his room. 'What's happened now in this tiresome case of ours?' he went on in a tone of exaggerated weariness, as Mendip sat down and lit a cigarette.

For the next few minutes, Orkell sucked at his pipe while Robin Mendip told him about Mrs Blaney.

'So the position is, Julius, that, unless it conflicts with your client's instructions, I hope we can keep Mrs Blaney under wraps to the extent that if she has to be called, her address and the name she's living under need not be revealed in open court.'

Julius Orkell removed the pipe from his mouth and laid it on the brief he had been reading.

'I don't wish to hammer the lady,' he said. 'We'll certainly have a word with the judge before the court sits on Monday morning, but I'm sure he'll feel that she must be called. After all, she explains what Fulmer was doing at Medina Towers. Her evidence fills in a hitherto yawning gap in the sequence of events. But I have no instructions to suggest that she had anything to do with the murder.' He paused. 'Not yet, I haven't,' he added, giving Mendip a despairing look. 'Of course, I can't say what Donig's reaction to the news will be.' He put his pipe back into his mouth and relit it amidst loud sucking noises and clouds of smoke. 'I don't mind telling you, Robin, I've had some awkward clients in my time and Donig is one of them. He says very little and I'm not sure I believe what little he does say. As you've probably noticed, the defence has a faintly improvised air and that's primarily on account of Donig's reluctance to get down to the nuts and bolts of his defence. I told him quite bluntly the other evening when he asked me how I rated his chances that I thought he'd be convicted. And all he did was nod. It wasn't a very happy nod, mark you; but that was his only reaction. It wouldn't be right for me to disclose the exact details of his defence – and I know you're not asking me to – and, in any event, they may be added to or subtracted from by the time he comes to give evidence, but his prime interest has been in finding out something about these names I've asked witnesses about.' He gave Robin Mendip a helpless smile. 'My personal belief – which, of course, has nothing to do with his defence – is that he shot Fulmer, but that it was a contract killing as the police surmise. And what Donig is anxious to discover is who put out the contract. As I say, it seems to be his only interest, not that it'll save him from conviction.'

'If he doesn't know who put out the contract, there must have been at least one intermediary.'

'Isn't that usual in this sort of killing? The chap who is paying the money likes to hide himself as far back as he can. Isn't that the way they operate? You know more about these matters than I do, Robin.'

'I think it often is like that,' Mendip said. 'But how does it avail him even if he does find out?'

'It doesn't, of course, and I've told him so, but I suppose it's a comfort to one in a prison cell to know that others as guilty as oneself are also locked up. When my instructing solicitor saw him during the lunch adjournment yesterday, he was on about this person Eric Bliss. He seems to have lost interest in Everett and Blaney for the time being.'

'I'm afraid I'm still unable to help you there, Julius. The police seem as puzzled as anyone. Can you get a physical description?'

'Naseby has told Donig to provide one if he wants the matter taken further. Not that it's likely to help much, unless this Bliss has three ears or some other distinguishing feature.'

Robin Mendip got up. 'Well, I won't take up any more of your time. Shall we meet around ten o'clock at the Bailey on Monday? That'll give us time to go and talk to the judge about Mrs Blaney.'

'I'll see you then. Meanwhile I'd better have a word with my instructing solicitor. Incidentally, the reason my junior's not here is because he has pranced away to do a case at Lewes.'

'Will he be back with you on Monday?'

'He'd better be!'

Robin Mendip chuckled. As he strolled back through the sunshine, he reflected that he was glad to be a member of a profession where you could still have an off-the-record discussion with your forensic opponent without fear of any advantage being taken by either side. Mind you, he could think of a number of barristers with whom he wouldn't have dared to talk so freely. Alas, too, they seemed to be on the increase.

Few members of the public realised the extent to which trust was the sole foundation whereon was built the whole working relationship between members of the Bar and between Bar and Bench.

* * *

Later that day, after darkness had fallen, Harry Everett cautiously approached his home. Luckily for him, he spotted the police officer, whom D.C.I. Michaels had posted to keep watch on the house, before the officer saw him and, quickening his pace, walked on past with head turned the other way. The officer gave him the merest glance and only subsequently, when it was too late, wondered about the figure whose walk had been more reminiscent of someone battling with a blizzard than enjoying a balmy night. By this time, Everett had vanished.

So they *were* looking for him. It hadn't been a trick to get him away from his home, but a genuine tip-off. Having a naturally suspicious mind, he had wondered at first, even though he had judged it prudent to get out. Act first and ask questions afterwards had always been one of his guiding principles.

Well, thank goodness he *had* acted or by now he would be sitting in the cell of some police station. Somehow he hadn't thought they would actually have a man keeping the premises under surveillance.

It underlined their determination to find him.

It also fortified his not to be found.

CHAPTER SEVENTEEN

Clare made her own way to the Old Bailey on Monday morning. Nick had said how important it was that she should be on hand, as, if Ella Blaney was to be called to give evidence, someone would have to go and tell her and persuade her to come to court. And Clare, he had pointed out, was the one person who had gained her confidence. He proposed that she and Ted Cambridge should go and fetch her and bring her to the Old Bailey.

This made sense to Clare and she accordingly agreed to ask Sally to collect Simon from play-school. Her conscience was eased by the knowledge that they were about to have Alexander for a whole weekend when his parents went off for a brief second honeymoon at Brighton.

Clare was aware that, in Sally's eyes, a C.I.D. officer's wife lived in a romantically exciting world which was better than many T.V. serials. She had so commented to Clare, adding, 'Though I'm glad that Tony doesn't call on me to help him in his work.'

Her husband, Tony, was a heating engineer who, on more than one occasion, had answered Clare's and Nick's cries for help when sudden disaster had threatened in the home.

'I can't risk being seen by Brenda Fulmer,' she had said when Nick had first asked her to come to court.

Nick had agreed that this risk must be avoided and, accordingly, it was arranged that she should go and await events well away from the court where the trial was taking place.

At about the moment when Clare was making a somewhat furtive entrance into the building, Robin Mendip and Julius Orkell, with their respective junior counsel, were processing along a thickly carpeted corridor on their way to see the judge in his private room.

After Mendip had explained the purpose of their visit, Mr Orkell told Mr Justice Finderson that it was not part of his defence to attack Mrs Blaney and that he was content that her anonymity should be protected in the way suggested by prosecuting counsel.

For a time, it seemed as if the judge was not prepared to go along with the idea. He stared in front of him with pursed lips.

'I never care for these hole-in-the-corner arrangements,' he said, at length. 'On the other hand the course you are proposing is undoubtedly a compassionate one. If you're both satisfied that it's also a proper course, I'll accept it as such. By which I mean, I'll accept your judgment of the lady and that she is deserving of such consideration.'

'I'm prepared to accept what the police have told me about that,' Mendip said.

'And I'm prepared to accept what my learned friend tells me,' Mr Orkell said with great gravity.

'Very well,' the judge remarked with an air of finality, 'I think the best way of dealing with her evidence will be if I allow you, Mendip, to re-open your case in order to call her, it being made clear on the record that this is being done without objection from the defence. That will enable you to examine her in chief and you, Orkell, to cross-examine if you desire. It shouldn't take very long if you confine her evidence to the bare essentials.'

'I'll have to, as she hasn't made a written statement,' Mendip observed, and immediately regretted having spoken.

'Why haven't the police obtained a signed statement from her? That seems to me most remiss.' The judge's tone rang with judicial displeasure.

'She refused to make a written statement and the police could hardly force her to do so. In fact I think it's to their credit that they got her to say anything at all. I gather it was very much touch and go.' Robin Mendip spoke in a mollifying voice and was relieved when the judge didn't pursue the matter further. So far he had managed to avoid mentioning Clare's role either to Julius Orkell or to the judge.

'If I put back sitting until eleven o'clock, will that give you time to get the witness here?' Mr Justice Finderson asked, in a faintly irritable tone.

'I'll go and tell the officer right away and he can send a car for her,' Mendip said.

So it was that, a few minutes later, Clare was sitting beside Ted Cambridge as he threaded his way eastwards through the City's congested streets.

'I hope to God she hasn't gone out,' he said, glaring at the passengers streaming off a bus which was blocking their way.

'Nothing we can do, if she has. Nick was going to phone her and tell her we were on our way.'

'That may frighten her off,' Ted Cambridge said gloomily.

'It's one of those situations where whatever you do may be wrong. It's no good fretting, Ted.'

When they arrived at Medina Towers, Clare left Ted Cambridge in the car and hurried into the North Block. For once, a lift was actually waiting on the ground floor with doors open. Clare dived in and pressed the button for the fourth. As she ascended she heard the next lift pass by on its way down and reflected on the irony should Ella Blaney be in it.

But a long couple of minutes later, it was Ella Blaney who opened the door to Clare's knock.

'Your husband phoned,' she said. 'I was just going out.'

Clare let out a silent sigh of relief. It could only mean she was ready to accompany them.

'Did he explain things to you?'

'He said I was needed at court, but that I wouldn't have to give my new name or address and that I would only have to answer a few questions.'

She spoke quietly and with the same natural dignity that had impressed Clare on her previous visit.

'The car's waiting, if you're ready, Mrs Blaney,' she said.

'It's not a police car, is it?' Mrs Blaney asked in suddenly anxious voice.

'It belongs to D.C. Cambridge,' Clare said, reassuringly. 'It looks like any other car. It doesn't have any sirens and blue lamps. And he's parked round the corner so that none of your neighbours will see you go.' When they reached the car, Clare got into the back with Ella Blaney and immediately began asking after her two children and their latest activities in an effort to keep her mind off the ordeal ahead, while Ted Cambridge wove a skilful way through the traffic.

It occurred to Clare afterwards that the whole exercise had been rather like rushing someone to hospital for an emergency operation. It was all over before they had time to think about it.

In the witness box, she acknowledged that she was Mrs Blaney, wife of George Blaney who was serving twenty years in Parkhurst Prison and that she lived at the address shown to her on a piece of paper under an assumed name. In answer to Robin Mendip's further questions, she said that Stanley Fulmer, who had been her husband's solicitor, visited her on the evening he was killed. That the visit was at his instigation and that its purpose was to dissuade her from pursuing action she had taken against him with the Law Society. She said she had no idea he was going to his death when he left her and that she had never seen or heard of the accused. Indeed, that she had never set eyes on him until this very day. Quietly, but with head held high, she explained why she had not told all this to the police when they first came knocking on doors in the area.

Nick, who watched her closely while she was giving her evidence, hoped that everyone was as impressed by her demeanour as he was. From time to time he glanced round the court-room to observe the reactions of others. Donig maintained his customary air of detachment, as though he found her evidence interesting but far removed from anything concerning himself, and Brenda Fulmer sat forward with chin cupped in hand observing the witness intently as though sizing her up for a portrait.

Nick wondered what she was thinking now that she knew what her husband had been up to that evening.

Robin Mendip sat down and Mr Orkell rose, but only to say that he had no questions to ask in cross-examination.

'Very well, madam, you may go,' Mr Justice Finderson said in a tone as frostily impartial as the top of a Swiss mountain. Whatever his private view of the witness, it was well concealed. He had insisted that Ella Blaney should be called, but, thereafter, he had shown her a chilly neutrality.

With the same air of dignified composure, she now picked her way out of court. As she passed close to Brenda Fulmer, the solicitor's widow turned away. Nick, who observed this tiny incident, wondered again what she was thinking.

Thus, half an hour after arriving at the Old Bailey, Mrs Blaney was being driven home again.

'Have you ever given evidence before?' Clare enquired, no longer feeling impelled to distract her charge's mind from the subject.

Ella Blaney nodded. 'But never on behalf of the police,' she said with a faint smile. 'I've always been on the other side. George'll throw ten fits when he hears what I've done.' There was a note of affection in her voice as though she felt as capable of coping with George's reaction as she was of bringing up their two children.

As they neared Medina Towers, she suggested that she should be dropped close to the shops. She had things to buy and would walk home. She shook hands with Clare and nodded a farewell to Ted Cambridge. Then getting out of the car, she walked away without a backward glance. Clare watched her go, hoping that she wouldn't ever have cause to regret her decision to become involved. Clare's admiration for her was immense, but she was still Ella Blaney, loyal wife of a hardened criminal. Nevertheless, she made Clare feel a sudden surge of pride in her own sex.

*   *   *

Mrs Blaney had hardly left the court-room when Mr Orkell wrenched himself to his feet and said, 'My lord, I call my client.'

Donig stood up, flexed his shoulder muscles and allowed himself to be escorted from the dock to the witness box, where he took the oath in an uninterested voice, watched earnestly by all twelve members of the jury and with rather more clinical attention by the judge.

'Is your name Clive Donig?' asked Mr Orkell and received a brief nod. 'Please answer the question. The shorthand writer can't record a nod.'

'Yes.'

'And at the time of your arrest in January, did you occupy a room at number twenty-eight Dorritt Street in North London?'

'Yes.'

'Are you twenty-nine years old?'
' 'Sright.'

He thinks he's back in the ring, Nick reflected as he watched him. He wasn't still for one moment. He constantly shifted his weight from one foot to the other and his shoulders weaved as if Mr Orkell was throwing punches rather than questions. From time to time he blew noisily through the nostrils of his squashed nose.

'Did you shoot Stanley Fulmer?' Mr Orkell now asked.

'Did I shoot him?' Donig retorted with a puzzled frown.

'That's what I asked.'

'No, I never did.'

'You've heard the evidence of the finding of the revolver in a drawer of your room. How did it get there?'

'Must have been put there, mustn't it?'

'Did you put it there?'

'No, I've said I never did.'

'Who did put it there?'

'If I knew that, I wouldn't be here, would I?'

Mr Justice Finderson's pen hovered over his notebook. 'How are the jury supposed to interpret that answer?' he enquired.

'What do you mean that you wouldn't be here if you knew who'd put the revolver in your drawer?' Mr Orkell asked with an air of exaggerated patience.

'Well, I wouldn't, would I?'

'Wouldn't what?'

'Be here.'

'Where would you be?' counsel asked, having the unusual feeling of being sucked into a vortex.

'I don't know, but not here.'

Mr Orkell took a deep breath. 'When did you first see the revolver?'

'When the police found it.'

'You'd never seen it before?'

'No.'

'How would someone have got into your room to plant it in the drawer?'

'Through the door, I suppose.'

'Does anyone have a key apart from yourself?'

'No.'

'Then how would someone have got in?'

'Must have had a key, mustn't he?'

'Without your knowledge, you mean?'

'Certainly without my knowledge.'

'Can you suggest to the jury who might have wished to incriminate you in this way?'

'That's asking, isn't it?'

'Will you please try and answer my question,' Mr Orkell said in a grating voice.

'What I mean is that everyone makes a few enemies along the way.'

'So you're suggesting that an enemy did this to you?'

'Looks like it to me.'

'And you don't wish to name anyone?'

'That's right,' Donig said in a tone of abrasive indifference.

'I now want to ask you about the money which the police found in your room. Where'd it come from?'

'I won it.'

'Are you able to tell the jury where you won it?'

'I just won it, gambling like.'

'All at one time?'

'No.'

'Over how long a period?'

'Can't say. Weeks. Perhaps months.'

'Where do you gamble?'

'All over the place.'

'Horse racing?'

'Sometimes.'

'Cards?'

'Sometimes.'

'Any other sort of gambling?'

'Dogs.'

'Yes?'

'That's about it.'

Mr Orkell pulled out a handkerchief and passed it across his brow. Talk about awkward and cussed clients, this chap easily walked off with first prize. He must be mental, even though the prison medical officer had not found that he came within any of the defined categories of mental illness. No sane person could be quite so belligerently off-hand in his own defence. It must be one of those cases of brain damage from constant clouts to the head when he was a boxer in the army.

Mr Orkell put away his handkerchief and once more faced his client, who was watching him with his overbright blue eyes.

'Were you anywhere near Medina Towers around eight o'clock on the evening of January the eighth last?'

'No.'

'Where did you spend that evening?'

'How do I know?'

'Because you must surely have given the question some thought,' Mr Orkell said with a note of exasperation.

'It was nearly six months ago. How can I remember now?'

'When the police first saw you, it was only two days after the murder of Mr Fulmer. Were you not able to remember then?'

'Yes, I told them I'd been out drinking that evening.'

Mr Orkell decided to leave the subject, feeling himself in danger of cross-examining his own client if he pursued it further. It was with considerable relief that he observed Mr Justice Finderson lay down his pen and gently massage one of his fingers. The court was about to adjourn for lunch.

'I'm afraid our client's not doing himself much good,' Mr Naseby remarked to his counsel as the court emptied.

'I don't know why he bothers to deny it at all,' Mr Orkell said bleakly. 'He might just as well plead guilty as behave in this brutish, couldn't-care-less fashion.'

'Yes, I'm so sorry,' Mr Naseby remarked.

'No need for you to apologise! If he's not disposed to help himself, there's nothing any of us can do about it.'

Mr Naseby shook his head in a worried manner. 'He certainly is a most unpredictable person. When I saw him over the weekend and told him about Mrs Blaney, he couldn't have seemed less interested and yet when I took that original proof of evidence from him, he was so insistent that Blaney and those other names be dragged in with the suggestion that they had better motives than he to have murdered Mr Fulmer. I really don't understand the man.'

'Nor do I,' Mr Orkell said briskly. 'Nor am I going to waste

the lunch break speculating about him. See you back here at
two o'clock.'

*   *   *

Sod the lot of them! So ran Donig's thoughts as he sat
eating his own lunch in one of the cells beneath the court-
room. Sod his fussy solicitor and pompous counsel. Sod the
judge dressed up like Santa Claus and only waiting to give him
a life sentence. Sod the earnest-faced jurors and their self-
righteous expressions. Above all, sod the prosecuting counsel
who was waiting to cross-examine him.

He would like to take them all on in the boxing ring, instead
of a fancy court of law. Then they'd soon learn who was the
best man. Then they'd get as good as they gave.

But as he'd realised from the outset, he had been well and
truly knackered. He'd walked into a sodding trap. He was like
a lion caught in a net. As time had gone by his struggles had
diminished and now he felt there wasn't much point in fight-
ing on.

And yet . . . and yet he must still have a friend somewhere.
Someone who had tried to square the jury, but had picked the
wrong bloke. That was a bloody disaster!

A mixture of gloom and indifference swept over him again.
He was resigned to his fate. Almost. And still the worst part
was not knowing who had knackered him; who had pulled the
mat from under his feet so that he had fallen helplessly into
the arms of the law.

Sod him, whoever he was, more than all the others put
together!

*   *   *

For over an hour when the trial resumed, Mr Orkell continued to elicit his client's evidence. It seemed for a while that
Donig had decided to be more forthcoming. At all events, he
and his counsel seemed to be less at loggerheads.

When Robin Mendip rose to cross-examine, the accused
faced him with screwed-up eyes and tensed body, as if daring
him to land a punch.

'I want to ask you first about the two thousand pounds in
cash which the police found in your room. Why were the notes

in careful bundles of a hundred pounds with a rubber band round each?'

'Why shouldn't they be?'

'Did your gambling winnings always come at a hundred pounds a time?'

'Of course they didn't.'

'Then explain why the money was found that way.'

Donig frowned angrily. 'I did it,' he said, after a noticeable pause.

'Why?'

'Why?' he echoed in a puzzled tone. 'Why shouldn't I?'

'Do you agree that the money in that box gave the appearance of having reached you exactly as it was found.'

'You can say that, if you want.'

'But do you agree?'

'No, of course I don't agree!'

Mendip glanced at a note which Nick had just passed him. 'Did you have to buy a supply of rubber bands?'

'No.'

'Where'd they come from?'

'I had them.'

'What? Precisely the right number?'

'How do I know?'

'Because no other rubber bands were found in your room, apart from those round the bundles of notes. What's your answer to that?'

'I've got better things to do than count rubber bands.'

'I see. Now I want to ask you about the unknown person who, you allege, planted the revolver on you . . .'

'Not much good you asking when he's unknown, is there?'

'If you'd just let me put my question, then you can answer it,' Mendip said. 'How could this person have got a key to your room?'

'There's lots of people walking around with keys they didn't ought to have.'

'Is that the only explanation you can give?'

'It's a good explanation, isn't it?'

'That's for the jury to decide,' Mendip remarked drily. 'You agree that someone must have wanted to frame you, if your account is true?'

163

'Certainly they did.'

'And you've no idea who?'

'Perhaps I have, perhaps I haven't.'

'Let me try and help you with names, names introduced into evidence by your own counsel. First of all could *he* have wanted to frame you?' Mendip asked, as the piece of paper bearing Blaney's name was handed to Donig.

'He's inside, isn't he?'

'So I understand. Then you don't consider him a possibility?'

'No.'

'What about *him*?' The usher thrust the slip with Everett's name in front of the witness.

'What about Harry?'

'You know him?'

'Who says?'

'You said Harry, but the piece of paper only gives his surname.'

Donig scowled. 'All right, I used to know someone called that.'

'Would he have wanted to frame you?'

'I wish I knew who'd framed me,' he said, in a suddenly vicious tone.

'Are you saying it might have been him?'

'You're just trying to trick me.'

'I'm asking you a straightforward question. Might he have wanted to frame you?'

'I don't know.'

'Is that your answer?'

'I've said I don't know. If he did want to frame me, I don't know why.'

Listening to this exchange, Nick had the impression that Donig was edgy and ill at ease. It was as if he didn't wish to believe the worst of Harry Everett, but was being swung to that view. Of one thing Nick felt sure, the truth lay somewhere out of sight of both prosecution and defence.

'What about Eric Bliss?' Mendip went on in the same conversational but persistent tone. 'Might he have framed you?'

For a second or two, Donig swayed to and fro on the balls of his feet while considering the question. Then suddenly gripping the sides of the witness box, he thrust his head forward and said, 'Yes.'

'Who is this man of mystery?'

'I wish I knew.'

'But you must know, unless he's an invention.'

'I don't understand.'

'Nobody seems to have heard of Eric Bliss apart from you. Tell us something about him?'

'What?'

'What he looks like for a start?'

'He's short and thin.'

'Go on.'

'He's gone a bit bald on top.'

'What colour is his hair?'

'Just ordinary. Sort of brown.'

'How old is he?'

'A bit older than me.'

'What. In his thirties?'

'Yes, but he looks older than what he is.'

'So far, you've given a description which could fit thousands of men. Does he have any distinguishing features?'

'His head's sort of narrow, like it's been caught in a vice and squeezed.'

'And how long have you known him?'

'I can't remember. Not long.'

'And where does he live?'

'I don't know. He never told me.'

'Where did you meet him?'

'In a pub.'

'Which pub?'

'I can't remember now,' Donig said, in an evasive tone.

'Well, perhaps you'll tell the jury why this man, about whom you seem to know very little, should have wanted to frame you?'

'He wanted me to do a job for him, but I refused.'

'What sort of job?'

Donig passed his tongue quickly across his lips and seemed torn by a conflict of decision. Mr Orkell was not the only person in court to freeze in sudden sharpened anticipation of the answer. The judge turned his head to fix the witness with an expectant look and the jury, too, all gazed in his direction.

'He wanted me to kill someone, but I refused.'

'Whom did he want you to kill?'

'He never said because I refused to have anything to do with it.'

'Why should he have approached you?'

'I dunno.'

'This man you hardly knew suddenly put this proposition to you?'

'Yes.'

'Did you ever meet him other than in a pub?'

'No.'

'You never took him to your room?'

'No. Not after that.'

'But if it was he who framed you, he must have known where you lived. Yes?'

'No.'

'How did he manage to get a key to your room and plant the revolver then?'

Donig's jaw dropped for a second. 'He must have followed me and found out where I lived.'

'But why? Why should he have done that?'

'To get his own back because I wouldn't go along with his plan.'

'Did he seem very upset when you refused to do as he asked?'

'Yes, he didn't like it.'

'And so you suggest that he got someone else to do the killing, but framed you?'

'I don't know whether he did get anyone else.'

'But he must have done if your story's correct, because he later planted on you a revolver that had been used to shoot Mr Fulmer. That's right, isn't it?'

Donig had a faintly punchdrunk air as he shook his head as if to clear it of muzziness.

'All I know is that I refused to have anything to do with it and I don't know what happened afterwards.'

'But you realise now, do you not, that it was the killing of Mr Fulmer you were being asked to undertake?'

'You're trying to trick me again.'

'I suggest that you agreed to kill him?'

'No.'

'And accepted two thousand pounds in payment?'

'No.' But the denial came as if his mind were elsewhere.

Robin Mendip sat down and the judge adjourned the trial until the next morning.

As everyone drifted out of court, Nick was left slowly gathering up his papers.

Donig hadn't been the only person to receive some body blows that afternoon, for he, Nick, was still trying to recover from a severe one, which had knocked him right off balance.

He now had no doubt at all that the description Donig had given of the mysterious Eric Bliss fitted Gordy Warren.

CHAPTER EIGHTEEN

Clare could see that something was wrong as soon as Nick came in that evening.

He went straight through to the kitchen, threw down his briefcase and gave her a look of despair. Gone, for the moment, was all thought of running upstairs to take a proud look at a sleeping Simon.

'Things are in a mess, Clare,' he said in a tone of utter gloom, 'one helluva mess and I just don't know what to think, except that I'm about to appear the biggest fool the Met Police have ever seen.'

'Tell me what's happened, Nick,' she said, gazing anxiously at him.

For the next five minutes he related the events of that afternoon and concluded with his now certainty that the phantom Eric Bliss was no one other than Gordy Warren.

'And do you realise all the awful implications of that?' he asked.

'It means that your informant in this case was backing more than one horse in the race,' Clare replied. 'And surely that's no great surprise.'

'It means much more than that. It'll now be suggested that the police allowed themselves to be gulled into accepting the word of a little twister who was simply using them for his own purposes.'

'Take a pace back and try and see events in perspective,' Clare said. 'It's not as black as you suppose. Indeed, it may even cast light in hitherto dark corners.'

'Persuade me,' Nick remarked, bleakly.

'Sit down and start your supper and I'll try to. While I'm dishing up, get me a drink, darling.'

Nick nodded. 'That's a very good idea. I'm ready for one, too.'

'As I see it,' Clare said when they were both seated with

plates of liver and bacon and fried onion rings in front of them, 'nothing that's happened necessarily reflects on the original tip-off you had from Gordy. It led you straight to Donig and evidence that he'd committed the murder. At the time you arrested him, Donig could give no plausible explanation of his possession of the revolver or of the money found in his room. What's more, from all I've heard, there probably isn't anyone in that court who doesn't believe he did it. All along you've been certain that it was a contract killing and that's the way the case has been presented. What has remained an unsolved mystery is who put out the contract. I'd have thought it a fair inference that even Donig didn't know. And if that's right, it means that there was an intermediary between the person ordering the murder and Donig, the man who carried it out.' Clare laid down her knife and fork and said keenly, 'In my view, it's a near certainty that Gordy was the intermediary. It explains why he was able to give you the tip-off so quickly. He knew first-hand who had shot Stanley Fulmer.'

'But why, if you're right, did he pull the plug on the man he'd commissioned to do the murder?'

'I can't tell you, but there must have been a reason. He had some old score to pay off.'

'In that case, one would have expected Donig to have been suspicious of him.'

'Donig only knew him as Eric Bliss,' Clare observed in a thoughtful tone. 'Maybe if he'd realised his real name was Gordy Warren, he would have been. There's a piece of the puzzle still missing and it must have something to do with Gordy's change of name for the purpose of this transaction.'

'So, on that assumption, the person who put out the contract approached Gordy and Gordy got Donig to do the job.'

'That all fits together,' Clare said eagerly. 'It's also a fair assumption that it was the person putting out the contract who murdered Gordy. It's not difficult to think of reasons. Either Gordy was threatening to give him away or was blackmailing him . . .' She paused, her eyes bright with excitement. 'And there's a further piece of the puzzle that fits. Assuming that Gordy gave you the tip-off about Donig on his own

169

initiative and not on the orders of the Mr X in the case, one can infer that, once Mr X rumbled this, he wouldn't have felt too secure himself. If Gordy could do that to Donig, he could do it to Mr X, too.'

'Not without revealing his own part in the affair.'

'Maybe not, though I doubt whether that would have been all that much comfort to Mr X. He would still see himself threatened.'

'But what about the fact that Gordy gave me the tip-off about Donig a couple of days after the murder and six months later he hadn't let out a mutter about your Mr X.'

'Yes, that occurred to me, too. The explanation could be that Gordy was quietly blackmailing Mr X and so wouldn't want to kill the goose laying the golden eggs.'

Nick smiled for the first time since he had arrived home that evening. 'You've really worked it all out, haven't you, darling?'

'Except who Mr X is.'

'And that's where I can contribute something. Scientific examination of that pair of galoshes we found at Harry Everett's reveals traces of mud identical with control samples taken from the towpath beneath the bridge. It also seems that the heel mark found is consistent with having been made by the heel of the right galosh. I had a phone call from Detective Chief Inspector Michaels just before I left the Yard this evening. So now the hue and cry to find Harry Everett is being intensified. X equals Everett.'

Clare frowned. 'Well, well,' she said in a tone that indicated her thoughts to be straying.

'I'm still not sure,' Nick went on, 'that when the whole story's known, I shan't look a ripe idiot.'

'Have you told anyone about Bliss being Gordy?' Clare asked, refocusing her attention.

'I told Mr Mendip. And Ted Cambridge knows.'

'What did Robin Mendip say?'

'He was his usual cool self. He simply said he'd think about the implications and let me know his view in the morning.'

'None of this can help Donig if the jury accept the prosecution's evidence,' Clare observed in a tone which seemed to lack one hundred per cent confidence in what she was saying.

'In theory, no,' Nick said. 'But you know what juries are where they sniff bad smells round the edges of a case. And heaven knows this case has enough rotten smells at its circumference. The last thing I want is Donig's conviction, followed by questions in the House of Commons, tribunals of enquiry set up by the Home Secretary and all that sort of procedure which only results in the police getting generally clouted by the media. If he's going to get out, I'd sooner it were now and not later. Even if he is as guilty as hell.'

Clare rose and began clearing away their plates. When Nick made to help, she motioned him to stay where he was.

'I can manage, darling,' she said. 'You get on with whatever you have to do.'

By the time she handed him a mug of coffee several minutes later, he had strewn the table with papers from his briefcase and was poring over a file.

Clare sat down and took a sip of coffee. Then twisting her head slightly she glanced at the front of a buff folder which was nearest to her. 'The Queen against Clive Donig', she read at the top.

It looked a slender file for all the work Nick had put into the case. Then she noticed the date on it, 1974, and realised it must relate to the case which resulted in Donig getting a suspended prison sentence for manslaughter.

Nick glanced up and noticed her gaze on the file. 'I've only just been able to draw that file. It was stored in some dark recess of the Met's archives and they couldn't trace it at first. I expected to be told it'd already been destroyed; not that it would probably have mattered. I only sent for it when Donig's defence began throwing up all those names.'

'I remember your telling me about it. He knocked someone down outside a pub and fractured his skull.'

'Yes. All I had before was the C.R.O. docket which revealed only the bare details. I did speak to the officer in charge of the case who told me a bit more. But that file only arrived on my desk to-day. I've not had a chance to look at it yet. Why don't you take a dekko?'

'You don't sound very hopeful.'

'I'm not. Pavement brawls outside pubs are a regular Friday

and Saturday night feature. They're all the same. But go ahead and read it. It'll save me doing so.'

Clare pulled the file toward her and opened it, while Nick returned to his own reading.

'Did the officer you spoke to tell you the name of the victim?' she asked suddenly.

'No, he couldn't remember it,' Nick said, without looking up.

'And what about the C.R.O. docket?'

'It wouldn't show it, only the actual offence. Surely you remember that, W.P.C. Reynolds?'

'I just wanted to be sure before I broke the news to you.'

'What news? Oh lord, what now?'

Nick was now gazing at her with a worried expression.

'The victim's name was Warren. Donald Warren. And he was thirty-seven years old at the time of his death.' Clare turned the pages of the short police report until she reached the penultimate one. She went on, 'Paragraph eighteen reads, "The deceased's only known relative is a younger brother, Gordon Warren with whom the deceased man shared a room."' She pushed the file across to Nick. 'So that's the missing piece,' she said. 'Donig killed Gordy's brother and walked out a free man. Donig was probably not even aware of Gordy's existence, though the name of Warren might have stirred a chord in his mind. Hence Eric Bliss's sudden materialisation when Gordy saw the opportunity of avenging his brother's death.'

'It looks like that,' Nick said, nodding excitedly. 'When Everett wanted Fulmer knocked off he used Gordy as his intermediary in hiring Donig. And Gordy ditched Donig as an act of revenge.'

'Would it have been generally known that Donig was a freelance hit man?' Clare said.

'Yes. The criminal intelligence people say he's known to be one, even though, until this case, there's never been evidence to connect him with any particular killing.'

Clare shivered. 'What a terrible occupation! Killing people for payment.'

'You certainly wouldn't need to have an imagination,' Nick remarked, 'and Donig hasn't.'

It was at the end of a further lengthy discussion that Nick said with a heavy sigh, 'The sooner Harry Everett's found, the better. Not until then are we going to dig out the remaining truth.' He gave Clare a rueful smile. 'I've never known a trial so embattled by extraneous developments. Heaven knows I want to see the end of the case and yet I dread to find out what else lies in store before we get there.'

The peace of the house was abruptly shattered by the telephone ringing. Nick glanced at his watch.

'It's after eleven. It must be your sister or your mother, you go.'

Clare left the kitchen to return half a minute later.

'It's for you,' she said, giving him a slightly curious look.

'Who is it?'

'A woman. She said it's urgent.'

'Didn't you ask her name?'

'No. I felt she wouldn't have told me anyway.'

With a fatalistic shrug, Nick went out into the hall.

'Detective Sergeant Attwell speaking,' he said warily.

'This is Olive Tishman. I do apologise for bothering you at home, Mr Attwell. Scotland Yard refused to give me your private number, but I looked it up in the telephone book. I recalled someone saying that you lived in the Barnes area. You do remember me, don't you? I'm Brenda Fulmer's sister. We met at the Old Bailey last week.'

'Yes, I remember very well, Mrs Tishman. What's your trouble?'

'I need to talk to you terribly urgently. It's about my husband and . . . Oh, I'd rather not explain it on the phone, it's all too difficult. How soon can I see you?'

'Do you mean to-night?'

'If I could. I'm so worried, I know I shall never sleep until I've talked to you.'

Nick could hear the note of hysteria in her voice.

'All right, I'll come round straight away.'

'Oh, thank you. You know my address?'

'I have it somewhere, but remind me. By the way, is your husband at home?'

'No, no he's not. You don't have to worry, he won't suddenly walk in.'

It seemed a rather ambiguous bit of reassurance, but Nick

was prepared to give her the benefit of the doubt her words had conjured up.

He expected Clare to raise a protest when he returned to the kitchen and told her what she hadn't already overheard.

Instead, all she said was, 'Hmm, that's very interesting. I'd been wondering about Frank Tishman.'

CHAPTER NINETEEN

It took Nick only twenty minutes at that hour of night to reach the block of flats in Mayfair where the Tishmans lived.

Olive Tishman answered as soon as he pressed the button of the intercom and he realised that she must have been sitting beside her end of it.

The outer door buzzed like an angry bee and Nick entered the foyer and took the lift up to the fourth floor. As he stepped out he saw Olive Tishman standing in a doorway opposite.

'I'm so thankful you've come,' she said, as she closed the door behind him and led the way into a large, opulently furnished living-room. 'I'm sure you'd like a drink. Whisky? Brandy? I think we have everything.'

'A beer, perhaps.'

'Yes, of course, I know there's some in the refrigerator. I'll just go and fetch it. Do sit down and make yourself comfortable.'

It was clear from her voice and her succession of nervous gestures that she was in a highly emotional state. She was wearing a pair of black trousers with a cream-coloured blouse and her hair had a mussed look without appearing positively untidy. Nick had also noticed a small bruise beneath her left eye.

She returned to the room and handed him a can of beer and a glass.

'I'll leave you to open it, as I always make such a mess when I try.'

Before sitting down she replenished her own glass from a decanter of whisky which was on a table with an assortment of bottles over in a corner of the room.

'This isn't just a sudden decision,' she said. 'I've been working myself into a state for days wondering just what I ought to do. And then to-night, I knew I had to talk to someone in authority and tell him what I'd discovered.' She took a sip from her glass and laid it on the table beside her. 'My husband is having an affair with my sister. When I say "is", I mean that he has been for the past year or so and it's still going on. I may say that I had no idea until Brenda herself told me last week. Well, she didn't tell me in so many words. She's much too subtle a person to come out with the truth just like that. What she said to me was that Stanley had had his suspicions about her and Frank and had told her so. She didn't say they were true, but it's become all too clear to me since that they were well founded.'

'Doesn't the fact that she did tell you indicate the contrary?' Nick asked.

'No. It was typical of Brenda to do it that way. Anyway, why do you think she's been going to the Old Bailey every day?'

'Why?'

'In case anything should come out linking her and Frank. If it did, she wanted to know exactly what it was.'

Nick gave a small nod. That certainly seemed to make sense.

Olive Tishman now went on, 'Of course, I taxed Frank with it and we had a row and he walked out. That was last week, and apart from returning to pick up some clothes he hasn't come back.'

'Do you know where he is?'

'Where do you think? With my loving sister, of course.'

'Do you know that?'

'I've rung her several evenings and each time it's perfectly obvious there's a man in the flat with her. I can tell from her voice and manner.' She made a mirthless sound. 'I've known my sister a long time. I can read her as clearly as the headlines of a newspaper.'

'Did your husband admit the relationship when you taxed him?'

'Not Frank. He just denied it flatly and struck me.' Her tone was bitter. 'But why should he walk out if it wasn't true? Mind you, I'm not saying our marriage has been all happiness, because it hasn't. Far from it. We've frequently rowed. Frank is a very domineering man. He has never been easy to live with. I'm quite certain he's had girls on the side from time to time. That's one thing, but to have an affair with your wife's younger sister is something quite different.'

Nick realised that this was where the shoe really pinched.

'And why have you suddenly decided to tell me all this? Not merely tell me, but send for me as a matter of urgency in the middle of the night?' He raised a hand. 'Before you answer that, let me tell you that I heard a rumour about your husband and Mrs Fulmer in the course of the investigation. It reached me in a form that confirms that Mr Fulmer had his suspicions.'

'Where did you hear it?' she asked sharply.

'I can't divulge that, but it didn't seem to have any bearing on Mr Fulmer's murder.'

'That's just where you could be wrong,' she said. 'That's why I realised that I had a duty to talk to you.'

Duty or the reaction of a woman scorned? Nick wondered.

'This man, what's his name, who's charged with the murder, all he did was point the gun and pull the trigger, isn't that right? Someone hired him to do it, isn't that also right?'

'Yes, that's still the police view.'

'And who did the hiring? Who wouldn't bat an eyelid about exterminating anyone who stood in his path? Who thinks that money can buy anything?' She paused, out of breath. 'That's right, Frank Tishman.'

A heavy silence fell. Olive Tishman watched Nick while she nervously revolved the gold bracelet on her right wrist. Nick, for his part, stared into the depths of his empty glass. Eventually, he looked up and met her stare.

'Am I right in thinking that you asked me to come here in order to tell me you believe your husband to be responsible for Stanley Fulmer's death?' She gave a small nod. 'And do you really believe that, Mrs Tishman?'

'I've only told you what I think you ought to know. I've been torn to shreds trying to decide what to do. But after the way Frank has behaved, I felt I had no choice. I'm not suggesting you should go out and arrest him. I simply thought you should know what I've discovered about my husband and my sister.' She paused and, in a faintly martyred voice, said, 'All I ask is that you keep my name out of it if you question Frank. Otherwise, you'll have another case of murder on your hands.'

CHAPTER TWENTY

It seemed to Nick that he had only been asleep a few minutes when he was awakened by the telephone ringing.

Propping himself up on an elbow, he reached out for the receiver on the bedside extension.

Although it still felt like the middle of the night, he could see daylight filtering round the edge of the curtain. And as if to confirm that a new day had arrived, a wide-awake and beaming Simon appeared in the doorway.

'Telephone,' he said happily, as Nick's hand lifted the receiver.

'Detective Sergeant Attwell?' a voice asked.

'Yes, speaking.'

'I have a message for you from Detective Chief Inspector Michaels. Will you meet him at Barnes Police Station in half an hour? Everett's been arrested.'

'O.K., I'll be there.'

He glanced at his watch and saw that it was three minutes after seven o'clock. At least, the station was only a few minutes' drive away, though that was a happy coincidence rather than thoughtfulness on anyone's part.

Meanwhile, Simon had turned the occasion to his personal advantage by squirming into bed with his parents.

Nick allowed him a brief frolic before pushing back the covers and jumping out. Clare had already disappeared into the bathroom, but now emerged.

'I'll get you a cup of coffee,' she said.

'That's all I'll have time for,' Nick replied, stepping over Simon who was examining something on the landing carpet.

'It hurt my foot,' Simon announced in an aggrieved tone, holding up a bristle.

'Go and put on your dressing gown and slippers and then come and help me get breakfast. Daddy's in a hurry.'

'Why?'

'Just do as I say.'

'My foot's hurting.'

'If you'd put on your slippers, you wouldn't have trodden on the bristle. Let me see your foot.' Clare gave the sole of his foot a quick examination, but, as expected, could see nothing wrong.

Placated by this attention, Simon trotted off to his bedroom.

Nick arrived at the police station at the same moment as D.C.I. Michaels.

'He was picked up in the early hours of the morning near the White City. An officer saw him asleep in a doorway and went to investigate. When he woke him up, Everett made a run for it, but the officer gave chase and caught him. I was phoned at half past two and I told them to bring him here.'

By the time he had finished telling Nick this, they had reached the small room which had been made available for their interview of Everett.

A few minutes later a uniformed sergeant and constable brought in Harry Everett. The sergeant departed again, but the constable sat down on a chair beside the door.

'I'm Detective Chief Inspector Michaels and I believe you already know Detective Sergeant Attwell.' Everett who was unshaven and looked dishevelled merely glared from one to the other. Michaels went on, 'I'm in charge of enquiries into the murder of Gordon Warren . . .'

'Who?' Everett said in a sort of surprised bark.

'Gordon or Gordy Warren. Or you may have known him as Eric Bliss.'

'I don't know who you're talking about.'

'I have reason to think you know something about his death.'

'Then you can have another bloody think.'

D.C.I. Michaels shook his head in a gesture of one largely reconciled to human obstinacy.

'What were you doing sleeping in a doorway last night?'

'It's a free country, isn't it?'

'But why sleep in a doorway when you have a perfectly good home?'

'That's my business.'

'It also happens to be mine,' Michaels said, in a suddenly

steely tone. 'In fact, I'd like to know why you suddenly left home two days ago?'

'P'raps you would, but I'm not saying.'

'And why you phoned your employer and said you wouldn't be in for a few days?' Everett said nothing and Michaels went on, 'You told him that something had suddenly cropped up. What?'

'I don't have to answer any questions. I know my rights.'

'O.K., you don't answer and I draw the necessary conclusions. It won't do you much good later on to say they're the wrong conclusions. Whose fault will that be? Many a bloke has gone off to prison because he failed to give a reasonable explanation when one might have been expected. Of course, I agree that it presupposes your having a reasonable explanation. If you haven't, then silence also won't help much, anyway.' Michaels leaned forward resting his folded hands on the table and giving the impression of a bank manager about to explain to a customer the ineluctable consequences of living beyond one's means. 'We know that you had a serious quarrel with Fulmer, the solicitor. From all accounts, he hung on to a large sum of money you'd left with him. I can guess where the money came from, but I can still understand how you felt when you realised you'd been cheated. You swore revenge when he refused to hand it over and threatened him physically. That's one part of the story, one might say the background. Now for the next part. You'd been associated with Clive Donig on a bank job in Croydon some years ago. You'd got on well together, which is more than either of you did with the others involved. So whom better to turn to than your old associate, Donig, when you decided it was time for Fulmer to wave his good-bye to this life. You knew that Donig was never averse to a bit of killing and he might even allow you a discount in the name of friendship. Except that you decided it might be safer not to approach him direct but to use an intermediary, so you probably didn't get the discount after all and also had to pay for the services of an additional person. Anyway, that was what you decided to do. And how you must have subsequently regretted it when your intermediary began to squeeze you for more money and still more money . . . until the day arrived when you reached another decision, namely that he would also have to be destroyed. And so, Harry, those are the two matters sticking to your plate at the moment. Being a principal in the first degree to Stanley Fulmer's murder and murdering Gordon Warren beneath Chiswick Bridge last Thursday night.'

'Is that all?' Everett said in a harsh, jeering tone.

'Probably not. There'll also be the question of trying to nobble a juror, though that's someone else's case.'

If D.C.I. Michaels had thrown this last comment out as a result of an overflow of confidence, its effect on Everett was immediate. He looked as if he had received a smart blow between the eyes. He gave his head a shake as if to clear it of popping stars.

'You can't pin any murders on me,' he said hoarsely, 'you've got no proof.'

'No?'

'You can't have.'

'I notice you say murders. What about the jury nobbling, are you admitting that?'

'What about a deal?'

'No deals.'

'If I fill you in on what happened with that juror, will you let me go?'

'No.'

'Then I'm not talking.'

'You've as good as admitted trying to pervert the course of justice and I have evidence that you murdered Warren. It's only a short step to proving your involvement in the death of Stanley Fulmer.'

'There isn't any bloody evidence. You're making it up. You're like all your lot, you just twist words to suit yourselves, you're a bunch of perjuring con-men.'

'Listen to who's talking about perjury!' Michaels observed scornfully. He whispered something to Nick, who left the room. When he returned a couple of minutes later, he was carrying a small holdall, which he placed on the table in front of D.C.I. Michaels.

'So, I don't have any evidence, eh?' Michaels said, fishing inside the holdall. 'Then what about these?'

With a flourish he produced the pair of galoshes, each one

sealed in a polythene bag, and held them up like a butcher displaying his best cuts.

Everett peered at them with a puzzled frown. 'What are they meant to be?'

'A pair of galoshes. And before you say anything further, I ought to caution you. Anything you say will be taken down in writing and may be given in evidence. Do you wish to say anything?'

'Whose bloody galoshes are they?'

'Yours.'

'Mine?'

'They were found in the scullery of your home and they bear traces of mud the same as that at the scene of Warren's murder. They also appear to have made a heel mark found at the scene.'

'Those are not mine,' Everett said with a mixture of anger and fear. 'I've never had a pair of those things in my life.'

'What size shoes do you take?'

'Nine.'

'Just the fit for these galoshes.'

'I tell you they're not mine. I've never seen them before.'

'Then how did they get into your house?'

'Somebody planted them there.'

'That sounds like the standard reply of someone who finds himself boxed in on all sides. Anyway, go on, who do you suggest planted them?'

'It must have been the bloke that phoned me. He said the police were about to arrest me for that jury business and that I'd better disappear for a bit.'

'And you did?'

'Yes.'

'Who was the person?'

'He didn't gave a name. Just said he knew all about me and what I'd done and wanted to give me a friendly tip.'

Though Nick now had no doubt that Harry Everett was responsible for the attempted jury nobbling, he was equally certain that he was not the Mr X in Clare's equation.

CHAPTER TWENTY-ONE

Nick reached the Old Bailey only a few minutes before the court sat. He managed to intercept Robin Mendip and tell him of the various overnight developments.

Mendip listened with a judicious air and then said, 'I don't think the judge is inclined to let anything interfere with the course of the trial. I've told him about your informant's death and his probably having been Eric Bliss and he takes the view that there is ample evidence for the jury to consider and that he doesn't wish them to be deflected from considering this case as an entity. He accepts that other people may be later charged in connection with aspects of Stanley Fulmer's death, but he's quite content to regard those as separate matters to be dealt with at another time. He pointed out that, for one reason or another, it's quite common for accused, who might otherwise be linked together, to be tried at different times. Finally, he can see no injustice to Donig in completing his trial.'

'What does Mr Orkell say about that, sir?'

'Surprisingly little,' Mendip said with a grin. 'As a result of his client's performance in the witness box, his heart seems to have gone out of the case.' Prosecuting counsel fixed Nick with a hard look. 'The truth is, Mr Attwell, that there *is* abundant evidence against Donig and none of these recent alarms and excursions has changed that. It doesn't matter how many other people were involved with him, if our evidence is accepted, he was the person who fired the fatal shot and that's all we need to prove to secure a conviction. And it's precisely what we have proved.'

Mr Justice Finderson's entry brought an end to the conversation and Nick slipped round to his seat in the well of the court.

The morning was taken up with a closing speech by Robin Mendip which was pithy and packed with punchlines and a much longer and more eloquent one from Julius Orkell, which was, however, short on facts. And when an advocate finds himself short on facts, he is apt to be correspondingly long on rhetoric. Hence Mr Orkell spent much time discoursing about the precious golden threads of British justice and reminding the jury, with a well-timed gesture of his hand, of the figure of Justice which graced the top of the very building in which they sat. Her blindfold, her scales and her sword were all dwelt on at considerable length.

When the court adjourned at one o'clock, the judge had just begun his summing-up.

As Nick left the court, he noticed Brenda Fulmer in her usual seat. She gave him a smile and a small wave and pushed past her neighbours in the row to reach him.

'Will it finish to-day?' she asked.

'I gather the judge will probably leave a few words to complete his summing-up tomorrow morning, so that the jury can go out fresh to consider their verdict. On the whole judges don't like sending juries out at the end of a day.'

'They're bound to convict, aren't they?'

'They certainly should.'

'I'm sure you'll be glad to see the end of it.'

'Except it isn't the end.'

'What do you mean?'

'We've still to discover who wanted your husband dead.'

'Well, don't look at me like that!' she said with a brittle laugh.

'I'm sorry,' Nick said, blushing.

'I should hope so. You gave me a look as if you thought I was guilty.'

'I'm sorry. I didn't intend that.'

'I'm glad to hear it. And to show that I bear you no ill will, drop in for a drink one evening when you're near my flat. Just give me a ring and I'll put the champagne on ice.'

'I'd prefer beer.'

'Don't be so literal. You know what I mean.'

By the end of the afternoon, it was apparent that Mr Justice Finderson had no doubts about Donig's guilt. He made his views quite clear to the jury, but then quickly reminded them that it was their view of the facts which mattered, not his. They should only accept his view, he added, if it happened to coincide with their own. Having outlined the principal facts adduced in evidence by the prosecution, he asked rhetorically, 'And what does the accused say about these important matters, his possession of the revolver and of that considerable sum of cash?' In a sceptical tone, which wouldn't be reflected in any transcription of the proceedings, he proceeded to read out Donig's replies to those telling questions.

Toward the end, he reminded them again that they were concerned only with the evidence they'd heard in court. Did it prove beyond reasonable doubt that Clive Donig had murdered Stanley Fulmer on the eighth of January?

'To use a cricketing metaphor, members of the jury, I urge you to keep your eyes on the ball. At one time or another, you may have had the impression that several balls were being bowled at once. You are concerned with only one of them. Does the evidence satisfy you that *that* man' – he jabbed a finger in the direction of the accused – 'murdered Stanley Fulmer? No other issue is involved in this trial. No other issue concerns you.'

When the court rose for the day, the judge had, as anticipated, reserved the final sentences of his summing-up until the next morning, so that the jury might have an unhurried deliberation before delivering their verdict.

Only Trevor Lee muttered darkly about judges' huge salaries and short working-hours. 'But what do you expect from a system that hasn't really changed since the Star Chamber?'

His neighbour in the jury box, to whom the comment was addressed, gave a non-committal nod, having no idea what the Star Chamber was and even less a desire to find out. Such had been his habitual reaction to Trevor Lee's abrasive observations throughout the trial.

His own experience as a first-time juror had been marred only by sitting next to such an uncongenial person. He foresaw furious argument and some bitter exchanges when they eventually retired to consider their verdict.

He mightn't ever have heard of the Star Chamber, but he recognised a guilty person when he saw one.

CHAPTER TWENTY-TWO

Ted Cambridge gave Nick a conspiratorial wink and pressed the bell beside the lilac-covered front door. After half a minute when nothing had happened he pressed it again.

Nick who was standing close to the spy-hole in the door was aware of a light being switched on inside and of an eye peering at them.

'Who is it?'

'Sergeant Attwell and D.C. Cambridge. May we come in?'

The door opened to reveal Brenda Fulmer wrapped in a kimono dressing-gown which she was wearing over the top of a pale green nightdress of some flimsy material.

'What do you want?' she asked in an anything but friendly tone.

'Oh, lord, sir,' Ted Cambridge said, 'we seem to have got Mrs Fulmer out of bed. What's the time?'

'I've no idea,' Nick replied, shaking his head.

'It's nearly half past eleven,' Brenda Fulmer said, frostily, 'and certainly no time for social calls.'

'Well, as we are now here and have got you out of bed, perhaps we might come in just for a few minutes.'

'I'm afraid not. I can't possibly let you in dressed as I am.'

'You look very respectably covered to me. Or is it that you're not alone?'

'Certainly, I'm alone,' she said, in a louder voice than necessary.

Somewhere out of sight a door was quietly closed.

'I believe there's someone in the flat with you,' Nick said.

'And what business of yours if there is? If you don't go away immediately, I shall ring Scotland Yard.'

'Oh, come, Mrs Fulmer, you're obviously trying to hide someone or something, so don't put on that sort of act. It becomes *you* less than most.'

Pushing past her, Nick entered the flat and went toward

the door he had heard close. He threw it open and gazed round a deserted bedroom.

The covers on the double bed were thrown back and the pillows indicated that two heads had recently lain there.

He walked across to the curtains and pulled them apart, but the window was latched and no one was hiding there.

He noticed a door which obviously led into the bathroom and was about to open it, when he was violently pulled away from behind.

'How dare you! How dare you come bursting in like this!' The words were accompanied by fist blows on the back of his head and shoulders, which ceased as suddenly as they had begun.

'Sorry, Nick,' Ted Cambridge said, puffing slightly, 'she slipped past me.'

He glanced at Brenda Fulmer's face which was transformed by fury as she strained to break free from Ted Cambridge's grasp. He turned back to the door and tried the handle. The door was locked.

'Come out,' he shouted.

There was a faint sound of movement inside, but the door stayed locked.

'Tell him to come out,' Nick said, turning to Brenda Fulmer. But she only spat an obscenity at him. 'Take her into another room, Ted, while I deal with this door.' When he was alone in the room, he called out, 'If you don't open the door before I count up to five, there are going to be some breakages to pay for. One . . . two . . . three . . .'

He heard a key turn in the lock and the door swung open.

Nick blinked in stupefied surprise. It wasn't Frank Tishman who stood with a towel loosely knotted round his waist, but Neil Penfold.

CHAPTER TWENTY-THREE

Fortunately, Nick recovered from his shock more quickly than Penfold who stood abjectly shivering in the doorway.

Suddenly, too, the last pieces of the puzzle seemed to slot into place. It wasn't Stanley Fulmer's brother-in-law who had been cuckolding him, but his junior partner. The inside man who obviously knew far more of what was going on in the office than he had ever wished to admit, including his senior partner's attempts to placate Mrs Blaney. Who knew about the quarrel with Everett, and who must have frightened him away from his house in order that he could throw suspicion on him for Gordy's murder? Who had his mistress attend the trial in case anything came to light which needed a thought-out reaction?

To every question, there now came back one answer : Neil Penfold.

Nick moved toward the man who still stood shivering in the doorway.

'You'd better put on some clothes,' he said. 'There'll be no going back to bed for a while. And when you do, it won't be this one.'

Penfold's shoulders sagged. At the same moment he grabbed a second too late at the towel which fell to the floor. Nick doubted whether he would ever again have a suspect in such a state of disadvantage.

'When did you first get to know Gordy Warren?' he asked, as Penfold reached down hastily to pick up the physical remnant of his dignity.

'In my previous firm. We kept in touch. He had his uses.' He smiled sourly. 'You're not the only ones who need informants.'

'And it was he who put you on to Donig?'

Penfold nodded. 'I never met Donig. Gordy made all the arrangements. I merely footed the bill.'

'And Gordy's bill went up and up?'

'When I realised it was he who must have tipped you off about Donig, I knew I was on an even slipperier slope. And then later Gordy's demands became exorbitant and I had to do something . . .'

'So you killed him.' When Penfold made no reply, Nick added, 'And tried to frame Everett.'

'It's no holds barred in the jungle. You know that.'

Penfold had almost finished putting on the clothes which Nick had taken off a chair and handed to him.

'Did Fulmer ever find out that it was you and not Frank Tishman who was having an affair with his wife?'

'Yes, right at the end. And do you know what his reaction was?' Penfold's tone rang with a mixture of indignation and disgust. 'To threaten me if I ever stepped out of line and didn't do his bidding. He said he'd make it his business to see I was blacked in the profession. That gives you a good idea of the sort of evil man he was.'

It occurred to Nick that there were very few people in the whole case who didn't reflect evil to some degree or another. Perhaps only Ella Blaney, who had emerged from the wings, held the spotlight for a short time and then left the stage to others.

And now it was Neil Penfold's turn to take over the leading role.

CHAPTER TWENTY-FOUR

The next morning, the jury retired to consider its verdict. After two hours, they returned to court and the foreman announced that he doubted whether unanimity could be reached.

The judge, after pointing out all the undesirable consequences of a failure to agree, urged them to go back and try again. But when after a further period, they returned and asked for directions as to a majority verdict, Mr Justice Finderson complied with their request.

Thereafter, it took them only ten minutes to reach a decision which was that, by a majority of eleven to one, they found Clive Donig guilty of murder.

Donig heard their verdict without any show of emotion, save for a funny little smile. To Nick, it seemed to indicate indifference to his fate. And this impression was confirmed when he heard later from a prison officer that Donig had become reconciled to spending the years ahead in prison once he had gathered that the man who had tipped the police off had met his own even stickier end.

Later, Ted Cambridge got into quiet conversation with one of the jurors as he was leaving the building and learnt that Trevor Lee had indeed been the stumbling-block to a unanimous verdict. He had made it clear to his fellow jurors that he regarded all police evidence as suspect and that went, too, for the various experts from the laboratory. He regarded Donig as merely the latest victim in a long list of police frame-ups.

When another member of the jury had said that his attitude seemed inconsistent with someone who had reported an improper approach, he had said scornfully that he abhorred petty bourgeois criminals just as much as the rotting fabric of the society in which we lived.

A few weeks later, the Director of Public Prosecutions decided that, given Trevor Lee's blunt refusal to make a written statement and support a prosecution, there was not sufficient evidence to warrant proceedings against Harry Everett for his attempt to pervert the course of justice. At the same time he also reached the decision that there was similarly insufficient evidence to sustain any charge against Brenda Fulmer, whatever suspicions might lurk as to her fore-knowledge of her husband's death. Nick had no hard feelings about either decision, though as far as Everett was concerned he could not help reflecting on the curious, if sometimes fickle, nature of underworld loyalties. It appeared that his attempt to nobble the jury had been the repayment of a debt to Donig, incurred when Donig was under pressure on a previous occasion to give him away to the police, but had steadfastly refused to talk.

On the day that Nick was apprised of these two decisions, he learnt something much more to his liking.

On arriving home, he dashed into the house and seized Clare in a bear's hug before she could get into the hall to greet him.

'Guess what, darling? My promotion's come through.'

Clare gave a gasp of delight. 'Oh, Nick, I am happy. That's wonderful news. Inspector, somehow, sounds less rustic than sergeant.'

'I don't mind about the sound as long as I get the money that goes with it.' He gave her a fond look and added, 'We'll be able to afford an extra something or other.'

Clare felt she had no need to enquire what he had in mind.